D1527800

# BURNED
## RETRIBUTION

NATASHA DEEN

ORCA BOOK PUBLISHERS

**Library and Archives Canada Cataloguing in Publication**

Deen, Natasha, author
Burned / Natasha Deen.
(Retribution)

Issued in print and electronic formats.
ISBN 978-1-4598-0726-6 (pbk.).—ISBN 978-1-4598-0728-0 (pdf).—
ISBN 978-1-4598-0729-7 (epub)

I. Title. II. Series: Retribution (Victoria, B.C.)
PS8607.E444B87 2015      jc813'.6      C2015-901712-2
C2015-901713-0

First published in the United States, 2015
**Library of Congress Control Number:** 2015935521

**Summary:** After a fire kills Josie's family, she is living on the streets
while she finds a way to bring her family's killer to justice in this fast-paced
entry in the Retribution trilogy.

RECYCLED
Paper made from
recycled material
FSC® C103567
www.fsc.org

*Orca Book Publishers is dedicated to preserving the environment and has
printed this book on Forest Stewardship Council® certified paper.*

Orca Book Publishers gratefully acknowledges the support for its publishing
programs provided by the following agencies: the Government of Canada
through the Canada Book Fund and the Canada Council for the Arts,
and the Province of British Columbia through the BC Arts Council
and the Book Publishing Tax Credit.

Cover image by iStock.com
Author photo by Curtis Comeau

ORCA BOOK PUBLISHERS
www.orcabook.com

Printed and bound in Canada.

18  17  16  15  •  4  3  2  1

*For Gudrun*

# ONE

It would be so easy to kill her.

So easy.

So simple to pass by her on the street, take her breath with the same ease I'd take her wallet. I've been on the streets for two years, and I've learned how to pick pockets and steal apples, which alleys are safe to sleep in and which ones to stay away from. I know which pizzerias leave their leftovers for the homeless and which ones watch over their garbage with the zeal of a miser guarding his gold.

And I know how to use a knife.

How easy it would be to bump into her. Instead of slipping my fingers into her purse, I'd slide my blade between her ribs, and I would whisper, "This is for Emily and Danny and Emma."

And she would look at me, startled, shocked.

And I would smile and walk away, leave her bleeding on the streets, the red stain of her life dripping from the smooth edge of my knife.

But I can't.

I won't.

Death would be too easy for her. A cop murdered on the streets. She'd get a hero's burial, and people would cry. The department would decorate her, and the police chief would make speeches about her *sacrifice and loyalty to the people she served*. Newscasters with their helmet hair would use their the-world-is-ending voices and talk about the need for better policing. People would rally for tougher laws. Cops would roust the homeless.

I live with these people.

They've been rousted enough.

I won't bring pain and torment to their already tortured lives.

Besides, if she died on the street, no one would know the truth of her.

The lies of her.

I will not kill her.

She will not die.

Not by my hand.

But.

I.

Will.

End.

Her.

Burn her. Burn her with the same heat she used to set my life on fire, and the orange-red flames that scorched the breath from my family will cauterize her soul.

# TWO

Head down, a worn baseball cap covering my hair and sunglasses hiding my eyes, I entered Tron's, a small family grocery store on East Georgia Street in Vancouver. The electronic bell dinged as I stepped through the door and left the fall sunshine behind me. My gaze flicked to the cashier. This time of day was the best for me, the worst for her.

People rushed in for milk and bread. The line of customers stretched six people deep and irritated-end-of-the-workday wide. In the back, at the ATM, was the kid. One look said he'd been born with some kind of genetic disorder. The stocky body and hands said he'd inherited the dwarf gene. But the larger-than-normal forehead said there was something else going on in his DNA. And the way he moved screamed leg surgery. Whether the operation had been an act of mercy or cruelty, I didn't know. And really, I couldn't allow myself to care. We all have our sob stories. The way he was dressed said the kid had money, at least; everyone in the store figured he was the usual rich kid, coming at the end of the day to drain his trust fund of some coin.

I knew there was more to him. I had seen the infinity tattoo on his wrist. I'd watched him long enough to know that, trust fund or not, the money he took wasn't from his account. Maybe I should've said something, but I had other things to worry about. I ignored him and, turning from his form, hunched in his private-school blazer, surveyed the crowd. I moved past the doors and kept casing the store. By the chocolate aisle, I focused on a guy with a goatee. One who didn't know me, but a man

I knew too well. A guy who was about to pay for a bad decision he'd made regarding my friend Amanda.

My gaze went back to the lineup. A man in a business suit glared at his vibrating smartphone, then scowled at the clerk, who gulped and rushed to finish ringing in the current customer.

Perfect.

This cashier was new. She didn't know to look up every time someone came through the door, didn't know not to be intimidated by the middle-class and middle-aged. I took my time, pushed up my hockey jersey and stuffed my hands in the pockets of the boys' jeans I wore. As a girl, I don't get baggy jeans. As a pickpocket, wearing pants big enough to hold three of me comes in handy.

I got to the candy and started grabbing chocolate bars, breath mints and anything else in my reach. Walking out of a store with a five-finger discount is all about timing and finesse, and I have both.

I overfilled my hands—almost. At the right moment, when the twentysomething-year-old guy with the goatee walked by me, I twisted, spilling the bars.

He jerked to a stop. Candy and chocolate littered his path.

"Sorry." I grunted the word, kept my gaze on the floor. Big difference between guys and girls? We chicks love to talk. Man, are we vocal. Dudes, on the other hand, not so much. It took my first year on the street to realize that if I was going to pretend to be a guy, I had to *shut up*.

"No problem," the man said and gave a short laugh. "You're hungry, I guess."

I shrugged. That was the other trick to being a guy. Men don't explain. They give information, but they don't give speeches. "Yeah." The nice thing for me is my voice. It's already deep. I scooped the chocolate bars into a pile—step one in my con game, with this guy as my victim and accomplice. The man crouched to help.

Perfect.

He blocked me from the cashier's view, and I'd already positioned myself so my face wasn't in the camera's lens. As the man handed me the bars and treats, I made a show of putting some back on the shelf and holding on to a couple of others. I made sure we bumped into each other as he moved to grab a bar and I went to put another back. I mumbled my apology, and he nodded. When he wasn't looking, I slipped two bars under the leg of my jeans and tucked them into my white tube socks. By the time we were done, I had three bars in my hand. He nodded at me, and I moved off.

Part one, complete.

Part two was trickier. I returned two bars to the shelves, then went to the cashier and waited in line to pay. This was the hardest part. Playing it cool. A few minutes' wait was all I needed. I gave it a couple of minutes, faked impatience, stuck the bar on the counter and left the store.

The hum of rubber tires on asphalt mixed with the chatter of pedestrians as I stepped into freedom. At the corner I hung a right and found the back entrance to Tron's. I knocked. Pulling the candy bars out of my socks, I waited.

A few seconds later the metal door opened. Tron was in his mid-forties, with graying hair that was wispy on top and a belly that spoke of home-cooked meals and a comfortable life.

"I wanted to Take Five." I showed him the first chocolate bar, grinning at my clever use of the chocolate bar's name in the conversation. "But I was worried I might be a Butterfinger." I showed him the third bar. "I think I Skored."

Tron rolled his eyes, turned and ambled down the narrow hall to his cramped office. I followed. The fluorescents buzzed overhead as we squeezed past shelves of inventory. "Did you pay for any this time?"

"Nope." I slipped my sunglasses off.

He grunted. "Suggestions?"

"Nah. She's new. She'll learn, but I'd add another camera by the soda section." I kept my sentences short, information without explanation. I'd never told Tron I was really a girl. Spending my time pretending to be a boy wasn't my favorite choice, but changing gender seemed the best way to hide in plain sight.

He grunted again and sat in the ripped office chair. "Usual fee?"

I nodded.

Bending, he pulled a bag of cans from under his scarred desk. "Soup, mostly." The light in his dark eyes softened. "Maybe a couple of chocolate bars and cookies."

The girl in me went soggy, but I held to my macho side and nodded.

"The people you collect this for. They're grateful?"

I nodded.

"Good."

I left the bars on his desk and grabbed the bag.

He cleared his throat.

Not moving my body, only lifting my gaze, I made eye contact and took in the uncomfortable lines of his body. "Yeah?"

"A couple of months back, you— uh—mentioned this girl you knew." He stopped, took a short breath. "She was having—"

"A small emergency."

"Yeah." He moved his bulk. His round face, and the kindness and softness in him, made him look like a panda cub who'd lost track of where his mother had gone. Tron sighed, then bent and tossed me another bag. "Just in case."

I didn't need to open the bag to know what was in it. I could see through the translucent plastic. Feminine items. There was a time his kindness would have moved me to tears. These days, I didn't think a jumbo jet could move my heart. I said, "Yeah. Thanks." I turned away from him.

He cleared his throat again. "Uh, you might want this too." Tron shoved a black box into my hand. "I don't know what's going on with you and this girl, but the streets are no place to raise a kid." He watched me for a second. "And you don't seem the kind who'd give up a baby."

"Yeah. Thanks." I shoved the box into the bag.

"Listen, buddy."

I hadn't given him a name three months ago when I'd first approached him about a deal: I'd occasionally steal from him to show the gaps in his security, and he'd pay me in food. It was a good arrangement. A sliver of clean honesty in the waste and mud that was my life.

"There are shelters, you know—"

I shook my head. "Price is too high."

Tron knew I didn't mean money. He sighed. "Look…just be careful, okay?"

I nodded.

"And if you need—if you need anything, tell me."

Two years on the streets, I'd learned fast not to trust anyone. Kindness always came at a price, and I couldn't afford the cost.

I liked Tron, but he had an agenda. We all had agendas. The trick was to make sure yours was the one people followed. "Thanks."

He didn't push the conversation.

"I just need to grab something." Leaving his office, I went into the store through the back entrance, to the ATM machine. There was a rack of boxed caramel popcorn, covered in dust. I reached for the box at the back, slipped my hand in and pulled out a cell phone. Good. It had recorded everything. I slipped it into my pocket and headed to the door.

Tron followed. If he wondered what I'd done, he was smart enough not to ask.

"Oh." I turned and dug into my other pocket. "A man dropped his wallet." I handed him the leather billfold of the goatee guy who'd helped me pick up the candy.

Tron stared hard. "He dropped it?"

"Right in my hands." I'd made sure of that. One thing I'd learned about being homeless was to look out for those who looked out for me. Amanda had been my protector and educator for surviving the streets. This guy had used and abused her. No way was I going to let him get away with it.

Tron closed his eyes and shook his head. Opening the wallet, he peered inside. "No cash?"

I shrugged.

He heaved a long sigh. "Where's the cash?"

"I honestly couldn't tell you."

"Look, I trust you, but if—"

"When you return the wallet," I said, "you should tell him that if he's going to rent people, he should pay for their time with money, not fists."

Tron jerked back, staring at the billfold like it was a snake about to bite.

I stepped through the door and he followed, walking with me to a city garbage bin. Lifting the heavy lid, he wiped the leather, then tossed the wallet.

"Can you believe how careless some people can be?" He shook his head and wiped his hands on his dress pants. "He should've been more careful." He gave me a final once-over, then turned and walked back to his store.

I slid my sunglasses back on. Then I headed to Hastings Street—specifically, the stretch that made up the Downtown Eastside, Vancouver's skid row. The dealers hadn't come out to play, and the drunks were still hunched in alleys, letting the hot rush of cheap booze warm their bellies. A few girls were on the corners. If their super-short skirts and thigh-high boots didn't tell passersby what they did to make a living, then the flat, empty light in their sunken eyes did. I went to my usual spots and handed off the cans to the old-timers of Hastings. Some of these guys were only in their forties, but life on the streets made them look and move like seniors.

Giving them food wasn't straight kindness on my part. Sure, for some of these guys, I stood in the gap between hunger and a half-full belly. The food banks were great, but for some of them you had to have government ID. And an address. Laughable. A lot of the people on the streets came here to disappear. They didn't want to remember their lives, let alone their names. Besides, there was more need than supply. A person could only visit the food bank once a week.

If I didn't bring food, they'd starve for the other six days, or dig through Dumpsters or go to the soup kitchens. The kitchens were the best option, except that charities run on the generosity of people with money. If people don't donate food and money, then those places don't have enough to go around. Too many nights, I'd had only my hunger to keep me company in the dark. If I could help even one person, then it was worth it.

But there was another reason.

The homeless had a network, a line of communication, a system of order.

Keeping in their good books meant that if I ever needed their help, it would be there. I moved through the network of alleys and sidewalks. For those with roofs over their head, a road was the thing that took them from one place to the other. For the homeless, the streets were a concrete jungle, complete with two-legged vipers, gold-toothed lions. Danger didn't lurk at every corner. It stood strong and confident, waiting for someone to do something stupid.

And that wasn't going to be me.

Not anymore.

I handed out the food and kept an eye out for Amanda. I wanted to give her the cash I'd lifted. She deserved it, and besides, walking around with two hundred bucks in twenties and fifties seemed a surefire way to get myself beaten up. The last time, it had taken three weeks for me to recover, and my ribs still ached when it rained. I didn't need another visit to a hospital, another "talk" with some nameless counselor who would fake compassion with empty eyes and an overly caring voice.

If Amanda was around, though, I didn't see her. Like oil on water, fear floated in my mind, always there, always reflecting back the questions I didn't want to ask.

After I finished handing out the cans, I headed to the East Hastings Community Kitchen. The facility was split into two sections. One had a kitchen and tables, and volunteers served dinner there three times a week. The other side was like a grocery store. Sort of. Shelves of food sat behind a long hip-high counter.

Volunteers were on one side. The clients were on the other. They gave us their family information and details on allergies, and we packed them a week's worth of groceries. The community kitchen tried hard to make sure all members got what they needed: baby food for the tots, prunes for the older folks. It was hit and miss, and the shelves were full or empty based on the community's generosity. Christmas was the best time. In summer, we all lost weight.

In exchange for helping to stock the shelves, I got food. Technically, the policy was volunteer once a week and get a week's worth of groceries. In my case, the organizers made an exception. I went there when I needed it and they gave me enough food to get by. It was safer. Too much of anything on the streets—food, clothes, money…happiness—and someone's going to come and rob you of it.

I got to the kitchen and found Clem glaring at a clipboard. "Where should I go?"

Clem was ex-military, bald with a ruddy face and wide chest. He'd still be serving Queen and country if a missile strike at his convoy hadn't taken out half his team and left him unable to reenlist. His gaze on his work, he said, "What's the rule?"

"How do you know I'm wearing sunglasses? You're not even looking."

"Don't have to." He stretched his thick neck. "Feel it in my bones."

I rolled my eyes.

"Don't roll your eyes at me." He scribbled on the page. "Off."

I took off the sunglasses and tucked them in my pocket.

He looked up from his clipboard. "Better."

"You seen Amanda?"

"Nah."

Crap. A wave of anxiety washed over me. Horrific images of what might have happened to her filled my brain. I swallowed. "You sure? She's never missed a day—"

"Since you've known her," he said. "She missed plenty before that."

Yeah, but the past few months had been different. And I knew why. "She wouldn't just go missing."

Clem shook his head. "Eventually, they all go missing." He impaled me with his stare. "Even you."

There was no judgment or meanness. Just the truth of the life I led. That we all led, though *led* wasn't the right word. None of us on the streets were leaders of anything. We were all just dragging our chains behind us and hoping the Vancouver rain would rust the shackles so we could finally break free.

He jerked a thumb to the left. "Go help that lady. She's new to the kitchen."

Yeah. I could tell. She was a fifty-something blond whose designer clothes said she should've been at a country club, not here.

I collected a bag of pasta, milk, butter—the basic stuff that would get her through the week. Then I watched through the window as she shuffled to an S-class Mercedes sedan. I wondered why she didn't just sell her $100,000 car but came up with the answer almost as soon as the question came to mind. In the neighborhood she lived in, it was probably better to sit hungry in the dark than have the neighbors ask why she no longer had a vehicle. Pride. It was full of empty calories and did nothing to fill a belly.

I finished my shift, and Clem found me at the back door.

"Here. A hero sandwich."

"Thanks."

"And something extra."

Frowning, I peered into the bag. Wagon Wheels.

"I saw you staring at them the other day—thought you might enjoy one."

My vision blurred with memories of the past, a time when chocolate-and-marshmallow treats could solve all my problems. If people's indifference left me wounded, their kindness killed me. It was too random, too unpredictable. There was no protection against it, and it didn't come often enough for me to use it as inoculation against a world that saw me as two-legged vermin.

God. I needed to get off the streets
before I lost everything that made me
human.

"See you tomorrow," said Clem.

"Tomorrow."

The wind coming off the ocean had
turned the night chilly. I tucked my bag
close to my chest and hurried down the
street. A sub and dessert for dinner. The
night before, I'd had some pizza that
someone had dumped in the garbage.
Tonight I wanted to eat by the ocean,
to savor the rare joy of eating food that
hadn't been pre-chewed, to sit and
watch the waves and pretend—just for
a minute—that I was a normal kid with
normal problems.

I walked down East Hastings to Gore
Avenue. At least, I meant to. As soon
as I approached the corner, my skin
flashed cold. I caught a glimpse of a big
bald guy with a two-headed-eagle tattoo.
It extended above the collar of his shirt

and encircled his neck. He looked up, stepped forward. The action cast a shadow over the person he was with, leaving him a faceless figure. Every instinct told me to run. Twisting on my heel, I did a one-eighty. A few steps away, I breathed a sigh of relief. Whatever was going down on the other side of the street, I wasn't the target.

Then I heard footsteps behind me.

Heavy, hard and coming up fast.

# THREE

First rule to surviving the streets: trust no one. I paid for that lesson with broken fingers and cracked ribs. Second rule? Show no fear. That one cost me bruised kidneys. The guy—those heavy steps could only belong to a dude—thundered toward me.

Option one: stop, turn and meet his gaze. But doing that was gonna mean losing teeth. Forget the hero sandwich. Bye-bye Wagon Wheel.

Time to run.

If I could make it to the SkyTrain, I could hop a car. No way was this dude going to outrun a train. Except the station was four blocks away, and even if I could get there, I'd have to hope there was one already waiting. Rule number three of living on the streets: *hope* is just another way to spell *dead*.

I tossed the food in the garbage and took off. No point in remembering where I left dinner. It would be gone when I got back. The guy behind me didn't call out as I took flight. Crap. His silence meant big, bad things for me. I upped my danger level from losing teeth to losing an organ. Couldn't let that happen. I was partial to my organs.

My lungs pumped the air, my legs moved like pistons, and my brain raced for a way to get myself to safe ground. Priority: get off Hastings. No one would help if I got in trouble here. Water Street would be good. Shops. Night traffic. And a couple of blocks down.

I dodged the people littering the sidewalk, skating close by them and hoping the bruiser behind me would slam into one. No sound of collision met my ears, but I didn't look back to verify his agility. My brain stayed three blocks ahead, reminding me of construction detours, closed streets and dead ends. I let my feet follow instinct and did a hard right on Carrall Street.

My ragged breaths and the constant slap of his feet behind me were the only sounds I heard. Which, as I raced across the street and ignored the don't-walk sign, was why I didn't hear the car coming at me until it was too late to stop or change my direction.

Before She burned my life, I had a home. Friends. Homework. Team sports. I rocked track and field, was a master at the diving board. When the dark sedan rocketed my way, my years of training came back. Avoiding a run-in with a car was a mix of hurdles and high jump. As the bumper kissed my knees, I leaped and landed on the hood. Perfect. The one thing I didn't take into account: speed.

The car rocketed me off my feet. I slammed shoulder, then face, onto the hot metal and bounced into the windshield. The driver, his eyes wide with terror, hit his brakes, and I became the rock in the slingshot. I flew into the air, and then gravity yanked me down. As I smashed onto the unforgiving road, I tucked and rolled. It felt like the impact cracked every vertebra in my spine, but I didn't hit my head. Stumbling to my feet, I hobbled to the other side of the street.

My body didn't ache. It howled in pain. Legs burning, lungs about to collapse, bones cracked. I paid the price because it gave me the distraction I needed. On the road, his car blocking traffic, the driver held on to his door, yelling at me to do something anatomically impossible. Behind him stood the bruiser, thick-necked, crazy-eyed, ham-fisted, pissed and unable to do anything. If he came at me, I was going to the driver and screaming for an ambulance, and the bruiser knew it.

I limped to a brick building at the corner of Powell and Columbia. A rattle from above made me look up. A girl dropped from the metal ladder. The ease of her jump labeled her an urban climber. She turned, made eye contact.

Nothing about the two of us was similar. I was taller, thinner and, because of my African-Chinese heritage, darker-skinned. But I looked into her eyes and was hit with the insane certainty that I was looking at my reflection. Instinct said she was like me: lost, alone, struggling to survive.

Then again, I'd just been rolled by a sedan and chased by a guy whose neck was thicker than my head. Maybe it was just the pain and adrenaline talking.

"Having fun?" I asked.

"Time of my life." She spun on her heel and ran down the sidewalk, her black hair spread like the wings of a dark bird as she ran.

I bent to catch my breath and ease the throbbing pulse in my back. Man, I was hungry.

And tired.

I pressed the heel of my palm to my forehead.

And lonely.

And freaked.

My pursuer was taking his steroid-fed body down the street, but the eagle tat was burned into my brain. The image originated in Albania and tagged him as part of a gang called the Vëllazëri. The word meant *brotherhood*, but *legion* was more appropriate. These guys made the Russians look like Boy Scouts and the Italians like choirboys. Whatever had gone on earlier, whatever he thought I'd seen, it wasn't going to cost me teeth or an organ.

If he ever caught me, I was going to pay with my life.

# FOUR

"You."

"Me."

Vincent leaned against the door of his apartment. His watery blue eyes took in the scrapes on my face, the bruises forming on my cheeks. The throbbing around my left eye said I was going to wake up to a shiner. "You look better than last time."

"You gonna let me in?"

"Why? So you can clean up, do a little presto chango, then bugger off until the next time?"

I'd met Vincent years back, when hanging with the homeless and ex-cons was a volunteer gig and not a way of life.

He was the only one—other than Amanda—who knew I was really a girl.

"You take off until your bones are broken or you're bleeding—"

"Not true."

"Yeah?"

I nodded, smiling even though the action sent a shock wave of pain through my muscles. "Last time, my bones were broken *and* I was bleeding."

He scowled. "Yeah, you play Ninja Turtles in the sewers—"

"I've never been in the sewers." Just the thought made my spine tingle. "You know how I feel about rats. They should stay above ground and in public office."

"—and I spend my time wondering if you're dead in a gutter."

"Aw, I didn't know you cared." I got a glare for that one. "We have a deal," I said. "Don't mess with it."

Another scowl. "Fine." He stepped back and ran his hands through his grizzled hair.

I moved into the worn apartment and grimaced. Vincent was into knickknacks. No. Obsessed with them. Ceramic milkmaids, dogs with bones…every cheesy figurine ever poured into a mold, he had. They were stacked on shelves, wobbled on the edges of his tables and crowded the coffee table.

"It's good you're here," he said. "I have some work." He jerked his pointed chin at the narrow hall. He gave me a once-over. "Hungry?"

Starving. I shrugged and didn't bother to hide the grimace of pain. "Yeah. I guess."

Vincent nodded at the easel in the corner. "Fix it. You good with ravioli?"

"Yours?"

"No, Chef Boyardee's."

"I'd prefer his. Yours tastes like wet cardboard."

"You could starve instead."

I grinned and held up my hands as though weighing invisible objects. "Die of starvation, or eat your food and have midnight cramps that make me wish for death."

His long face fell into serious lines. "Milk too. Right?"

I ignored the sudden lump in my throat. He was the only one whose kindness didn't make me feel weak. "Whatever."

"Think I got some Flintstones vitamins around here somewhere."

"I'm not ten."

Vincent took a step toward the kitchen, then looked back. "Prove it. Work and earn your dinner."

Long ago, he'd seen my art and called me a savant. Maybe. I just called myself passionate about the craft. I went to the covered easel and flipped up the cloth. "Bazille."

"Always a favorite with the illegal art crowd."

"Didn't one of his paintings sell for three million?"

"Four."

The carpet and walls muffled the sound of his voice, and I had to strain to hear.

"Can you fix it?"

I bent to inspect the paints and canvas, breathing through the pulse of my protesting sore muscles. "It's good. It could almost pass for his work." Before my life was taken from me, I'd been an average kid. Almost. I loved art. Loved everything about it. Thanks to art camps, the fine-arts program at Lord Byng Secondary School, student rates at museums and the Discovery Channel, I'd inhaled all the knowledge I could about visual arts. These days I got my art fix via the books at the public library and the rare visit to Youth Unlimited's Creative Nights.

"*Almost* is the word. I have to get it to Munich by next week. The owner's going to claim to find it in an attic." That was our deal. Vincent gave me the chance to remember who I used to be.

In return, I helped him fake paintings. He fenced the forgeries and gave me a cut of his take, which I appreciated. But until I got justice for my family, no way was I going to spend the money and live some soft life.

I sank to my knees, holding my breath against the pain. "The strokes are off in the lower left. Not sure about the formation of the flowers, the color on the—"

"Make it perfect. Then sign it—and none of your secret identifying markers this time."

"An artist always needs to mark his work."

"Only Bazille's signature."

"Yeah, yeah," I said. "No additions. Got it."

"Here."

I jumped as his voice sounded right behind me.

"Painkillers and milk. Dinner will be out in a bit. Drink. Eat. Paint. Shower."

He waggled a crooked finger at me. "In that order."

Three hours later, with enough pain medication to put down a horse and sufficient vitamins to live forever, I straightened. "Done."

"Good. Food's staying down?"

"Yeah."

"You seemed to enjoy it."

"Ate to be polite."

"Four helpings?"

"The first one needed company."

"That's two."

"What if they fought? Had to have another piece."

"Three."

"Odd numbers are never good."

"Right."

I stood. "Shower."

"Still in the same place it was last time." He kept his eyes on the canvas. "Hey, kid."

"Yeah?"

"Take your time. Water bill's paid."

I didn't say anything; I didn't need to. Vincent knew all about sink baths in gas stations, washing up in fast-food restaurants. Thirty minutes later, smelling like soap and not street, I wrapped a towel around me and went into the room he kept for me. Vincent was already there, riffling through the closet.

"Still want to be a boy?"

"Yeah."

"Rapper clothes again?"

"For now, but I need a second boy outfit."

He jerked from his position. "What happened?"

"Nothing. Time to change identities."

Vincent cussed long and hard. "What happened?"

"A soldier with the Vëllazëri thinks I saw something go down."

That got another string of cusses. "You're not going anywhere tonight!"

"Oh, okay." I let sarcasm ooze over my fear. "I should stay here with a convicted art forger who's still on probation and subject to surprise inspections."

He tossed me jeans and a shirt and focused on my long hair. "I got a blond wig you can use."

"With my skin color? I'll stand out."

"Exactly. Hide in plain sight." He rose, his arthritis making his movements slow and pained. "Dress."

He left. I scanned the pile of clothes— stuff for girls and guys. After tossing a layer of rap guy on my body, I put a chick outfit in the bag and followed that with a second dude outfit. When I came out, Vincent jerked his thumb at the easel. "It looks good."

"It looks perfect."

"Usual payment?"

I nodded. "Offshore." That was the nice thing about having a felon for a friend—he knew how to hide my money.

"Don't know why you don't take a cut of the profits. Get off the street."

"And miss out on all the glamor?"

He scowled.

I shrugged. We both knew why I was on the street. I couldn't do it—live in a comfortable house with money and clothes while my family rotted in their graves, cursed by the lies she'd told.

"Here." He handed me food. Then he gave me a plastic container of pasta. "Consider it a bonus."

"I'll see you later."

"How long?"

"Not as long as last time."

"Promise?"

"Yeah." I went to the door and wished him a good night.

He snorted, then folded his arms across his chest and watched me as I started down the hallway to the exit. Four steps later, the sixth sense that had kept me alive for the past two years went on high alert.

Crap.

What was on the other side of the door? No way could it be the guy who had been chasing me. I'd made sure he was gone before I'd set out for Vincent's. I turned the knob, slow and steady, then opened the door to the stairwell and walked into my nightmare.

# FIVE

Meena Sharma.

Through the window in the stairwell, I saw her step out of her sedan.

Calm.

Confident.

Stone-cold killer.

Spinning, I took two giant steps, slammed through the doorway out of the stairwell and into the hallway, passed Vincent, still standing outside his door, and headed for the back exit.

"Hey! Kid—what's going on?"

No time for talk. It was all about survival.

I crashed through the rear door and skidded to a stop. A couple of cops coming up the stairs. My heart slammed against my ribs. I rushed back to Vincent's apartment, pushed him inside and closed the door behind me. "Told you that you'd see me again soon."

"What's going on?"

"Meena."

One word was all it took. His face went slack, white. He cursed, low and vicious.

Rage made me see two of him, made the world blur at the same time it sharpened every edge. I didn't want to hide from the one who'd slaughtered my family. I wanted the fight, wanted to slam my fist into her round face and come away with her blood on my knuckles. But not now. Not here, when cops and guns came with her. Not when she could shoot me down and lie to the world.

"She may not be here for you."

We made eye contact.

"Yeah," he said. "I don't buy it either. The closet. Now."

Through the walls, Meena's footsteps sounded, coming ever closer. I yanked open the closet door and fumbled past the clothes for the compartment in the wall. If I squeezed my shoulders together, there was enough space to hide. Vincent locked me in the vertical coffin just as the knock boomed at the door.

"Yeah—"

I heard his muffled voice.

"—I'm coming."

"Mr. Pyra."

There was a time I'd liked her. Adored her and her daughter. But now? God, I hated her voice, and I despised the thought of her. Smug. Confident. A mass murderer cloaking herself in the skin of a protector.

"Congratulations," said Vincent. "You got my name right. You must be so proud." He paused. "I'd ask who you are and what you want, but you have the smell of bacon all over you." Another pause. "And powdered sugar. Isn't sugar bad for pigs?"

She chuckled.

"If you're checking up on me, talk to my parole officer. I've been a model citizen."

"We're not here for you, Mr. Pyra."

"I'm crushed."

I took a shallow breath. With less than an inch between the plywood and my nose, I wasn't sure how much air I had and how long it would have to last.

"We have reports of a young man entering your building."

I allowed myself a small breath. A boy. Not a girl.

"So?"

"He's wanted in connection with a traffic accident."

"He hit somebody?"

"Someone hit him."

"Let me get this right." Vincent was amused. "You're going door to door in this building, trying to track down a victim who walked away? You guys run out of murderers to find? I got a plugged sink I need help with, if you're looking for work."

She answered, but I lost the conversation because I was trying to figure out how she'd tracked me.

Then I realized how she'd done it. The security cameras on the streets. I was always careful around them, but my run-in with Eagle Man had made me rash. Note to self: Don't be a moron when in danger. And remember that cops can gain access to the cameras faster than you think.

"—waste your time."

Vincent's voice pulled me back to the conversation.

The creak of the chair shifting under someone's weight preceded Meena's response. "You and I have been in the system too long to play games, so I'm going to level with you."

"Wow." His contempt made the word heavy. "Should I make popcorn and we can paint each other's nails while you spill your guts?"

"Two years ago. You remember that woman and her two kids who died?"

The ice was on my skin, frozen memories of that night, of the flames that burned the heart from me.

"Lots of women and kids die," said Vincent, and I gave him credit for keeping his voice steady.

There was no room for me to move or shift my weight. I wiggled my toes and fingers, trying to keep the blood circulating and prevent myself from passing out. My shoulders ached, and coupled with the pain from the car accident, I was in a world of agony so bad I felt it in my hair. But it was nothing compared to my sharp, pointed rage as I listened to her talk about my family.

"Her ex-boyfriend shot them, torched the house." She paused. "We're still looking for him."

The image haunted my dreams; the unanswered questions tormented me.

Who had she shot first? Had Danny screamed? Did Emily cry? Mom would've thrown her body in front of both of them. I wanted to wail. There had never been a boyfriend—never been an ex-boyfriend. There had only been Meena, lying about a phantom lover to cover her tracks.

"Unless you want me to partner with a witness and give you a sketch of this guy," said Vincent, "I can't help you."

"He had an accomplice," she said. "That woman? She had been my house-keeper for four years. We shared stories about our kids. She helped change my daughter's diapers."

*Yeah. And you shot her in return for her loyalty and hard work.* I held on to my fury. It was better than diving into the grief.

"Most cases go cold in forty-eight hours, but not this one. Not for me. It stays hot. I'm going to find the guy and his partner, and I will bring them to justice."

"An accomplice?" Vincent snorted. "How do you know? You can't find him—

you can't even find some guy who got hit by a car."

"We have video."

"Of the hit and run?"

"Of the fire."

My heart slammed against my ribs.

"And I saw the hit and run. I never forget how perps move, Mr. Pyra. It's the same guy, and I'm going to find him. Bring him to justice."

How I'd moved the night of the fire was no longer how I moved now. Back then I was a girl. Now I was living life as a boy. Girls move from the hips. Guys from the shoulders. My run-in with the gangbanger must've made me forget my training. One stupid mistake, and Meena had me in her sights. I stopped breathing and hoped Vincent would keep control.

"What kind of video?"

*Way to go, Vincent. Way to stay in control.*

"Now you're interested?"

"Because I think you're full of fertilizer."

"YouTube. Someone taped the fire. Isn't it great living in the modern age? Private citizens tape crimes, and thanks to Google Alerts, I get updates on anything I'm interested in. And I'm very interested in the fire and this guy."

"Video, huh? Let me see."

*Nice play, Vincent.* I kept wiggling my fingers and used the memory of my dead family as a painkiller for my screaming muscles.

"Sure." Confidence was in Meena's voice. "Give me your phone."

"Nice try. Do it on yours."

There was silence, and I guessed she was calling up the YouTube video.

"You can't tell much," Vincent said after a minute. "That could be anybody."

"It's a clue." The words slithered from her mouth. "I don't like unsolved cases. And I don't like men who murder women and children."

God, I wanted to vomit.

On her.

Poor Emily. A street kid I'd befriended during one of my volunteer stints. She'd educated me about life on the streets. I'd convinced her to come off them, to get into the system. She'd been at my house that night to sleep over. We were going to find her a social worker the next day. If she hadn't been there that night, they wouldn't have mistaken her body for mine. She'd be alive, and I'd be dead. My mom's trust in Meena may have gotten her and Danny killed. But Emily's death was all on me.

"Your friend isn't a good guy." The chair squeaked. Probably her standing up.

"I don't have friends like that, but even if I did, he can't be that much of a threat. After all, you came to my apartment alone."

"The boys are outside. He's a bad guy." She paused. "But I'm dangerous." Another pause. "Not just to him."

I imagined her staring Vincent down.

"I'm deadly to anyone who gets in my way. We have officers canvassing the apartments. He murdered a six-year-old boy, shot him down—"

It took everything in me to stay quiet. For the first time, I was grateful for the coffin I was trapped in, because it was the only thing keeping me upright.

"—every cop in Vancouver wants him. He did a good job of trying to stay out of the cameras," she said, "but we know where all the convicts live. It's a matter of *when* not *if* we'll get him. If he's your friend—"

"Told you. I'm not friends with murderers."

"—tell him to surrender. No one wants a shootout."

Late at night, hunkered in a cardboard box and watching the rain turn my hut into sludge, I'd occasionally wondered if I'd done the right thing in never going to other cops and telling my story. Hearing

her talk about killing me in plain sight…
yeah, I'd made the right decision.

"Do the right thing, Mr. Pyra." The
door opened, closed.

A few minutes later Vincent cracked
the lock, and I stumbled into the light,
holding on to him for support.

"You have to leave Vancouver," he
said.

"Not till I'm done with her."

"She's got a video."

"You said no one can identify me."

His face crumpled with irritation.
"Sure, the video's mostly shadow and
movement, nothing else. Some kid
running down the street. But she won't
give up, Jo. As long as you're out there,
you're a threat."

"Good."

"There's software, algorithms she can
run…"

I scowled. "That's television fiction.
Most departments can't afford that kind
of equipment."

He tried to stare me down.

"Let me see it."

Vincent pulled out his phone and went to YouTube.

I watched as he typed in *arson*, *Vancouver* and *dead family*. A bunch of videos came up.

"This is the one," he said as he clicked the link.

I watched the video, then handed the phone back. "If she'd been able to clean it up and see anything that would identify me, she wouldn't have been here. She's got nothing."

"Run, Jo, and run hard."

I shook my head, ignored the pleading in his voice. "Someone has to make her pay."

"She's going to kill you. Whatever your mom saw her do, it's going to cost your life."

I shook my head again. "She can't get away with this. I won't let her."

Fear for me pinched his face, pulled his skin taut. "Don't be stupid. She's got the guns and loyalty of every cop on the force. All she has to do is call you a child killer and they'll pump you so full of metal you'll set off detectors in the next province!"

"She set fire to my family. I'm going to end her." I met his gaze, pretending not to see his terror. "I promise it'll be fine."

"You promise."

"I've never lied to you, have I?"

He sighed. "No, you never have."

I stood. "I know exactly what I need to do." What I didn't tell him was I only had two hours to get it done, and if I was wrong, it was going to burn me.

Permanently.

# SIX

Between the rattle of the SkyTrain, my injuries and the walk, I should've been dead tired by the time I got to Meena's house. But as the train pulled into its stop in the New Westminster suburb she lived in, all I was thinking about was my family. My hate took the edge off the cold wind, and my muscles vibrated with the desire—no, the need—to make her pay for what she'd done. I got to her house on Gifford Street, took in the quiet slumber of the neighborhood.

My family was forever sleeping in three cemetery plots. They'd never need light, never crave a soft bed or blankets still warm from the dryer. I couldn't bring them back, but I could—and would—make Meena pay for taking them from me. Stealing her laptop had never been a priority. It was too risky. She was bound to screw up someday, and taking a turtle approach—slow and steady—seemed the best strategy. I'd used the homeless network to keep tabs on her. So far, they'd only been able to bring me word of minor infractions, nothing I could take to the news.

Now, thanks to some random neighbor who'd decided to record the fire, Meena had video of someone running from the house. She had a solid record for closing cases, and I was the ultimate loose end. I was a target, but no way was I going to be prey. I needed to take the risk, get in her house and get the evidence I needed to put her away. I took the tools from my pocket and headed up the stone path to her front door. Bending, twisting my body so the light hit the lock, I slid the tension wrench into the lower opening, turned and held it steady, then slid the pick into the lock.

"Are you totally stupid?"

I jerked upright, pulling the muscles in my back. Whipping around, I saw the girl—the urban climber from earlier that night. "What the—how did you get here?"

"With my feet, newb."

"An urban climber, walking? Shouldn't you be swinging from a web?"

"That's Spider-Man."

"This can't be a coincidence." I folded my arms across my chest, palming the lockpick. "Are you following me? What do you want?"

She snorted. "Watching grass grow would be more interesting than following you. Anyway, don't be stupid. It's a prime neighborhood. Why wouldn't we both end up here?" Her gaze swept the street.

So did mine. No way was she here for a night of buildering.

"It's got choice pickings."

Stealing made more sense for why she was here, but I wasn't thrilled with her tone. And I didn't like her pet name for me. I'd had enough. Must have been the adrenaline from earlier that had made me feel like she and I were kindred spirits. "Fine. Go away."

"What are you doing?"

"Setting up for a game of checkers. What does it look like?"

"Looks like you're getting ready to get arrested for attempted B and E." She paused. "That's breaking and entering."

I gritted my teeth. "Yeah, I managed to puzzle that one out."

"So? What's going on?"

"None of your business."

"It is if you get us caught." She came up the steps.

"Us?" I looked around. She couldn't be alone, and I didn't know if that was good or bad news for me. "You have a team looting the houses here?"

She didn't answer. Instead she said, "Did you even check to see if the house is alarmed?"

"I'm not stupid."

"You are if you're breaking in through the front door."

I wasn't in the mood to explain why I knew all about the house setup but figured if I didn't give her something, she'd never leave me alone. "Thanks for the tip, but you notice the trees cover me. Go away." I pushed past her, stepped down the stairs and headed to the back door.

"You don't have any bags. No car."

"No wonder you're a climber. Talk about eagle eyes."

"Spotted your sorry attempt to play cat burglar from a hundred feet, didn't I?"

I didn't say anything.

She sighed. "I'll keep watch."

"Why?"

"'Cause if I don't, you'll ruin the neighborhood for the rest of us. I'll give you a signal if anyone comes your way."

"What's the signal?"

"Me screaming, 'Run!'"

That made me laugh. "Fair enough."

We got to the back. Usually, I can pick a lock in under ten seconds. Having her around made it take longer. Still…"See?"

She shrugged. "I'm beside myself, I'm so impressed."

I rolled my eyes and stepped into the quiet house. Despite what Climber Girl thought, I had broken into houses before. To fulfill the deal with Vincent, I'd done copies of art, gone into the homes and replaced the originals with my replicas. I had rules about which homes and which pieces of art I'd take. I would only steal paintings that were already stolen, and Vincent respected that.

Climber Girl followed me through the door and into the kitchen. "You're lucky they don't have an alarm system."

Luck had nothing to do with it. Meena was arrogant, too full of herself to think someone would break into her place.

A couple of times, I'd helped my mom clean houses, and the memories of this house's layout came flooding back.

"Hey!" Climber Girl's voice hissed my way. "You sightseeing or shopping?"

"Stay here. Watch the door."

I pulled a tiny flashlight from my pocket and panned it around the kitchen. No laptop. I aimed the beam at the living room. It washed over a rocking horse, princess castle and enough pink toys to put me off the color for the rest of my life.

"Get what you need and get out."

I jumped at the sound of Climber Girl's voice. She stood less than a foot behind me. "I thought you were keeping watch."

"You seem like you need supervision." She moved to the fridge and opened the door. "Geez. There are enough meds in here to start a pharmacy." She leaned in and read the name on a prescription label. "Dollie Sharma."

Never understood why Meena named her kid after a possession, but Mom had loved the baby. She'd loved both of them. "Close the door—you're letting out the light."

"I'm hungry." She pulled a soda from the door, then wiped her fingerprints off the fridge's surface. "And thirsty."

I rolled my eyes—which seemed like it was going to be a constant thing around this chick—and went back to looking for the computer. It was by the fireplace, charging. "Got it." I grabbed it, slid it into my bag, then went out the door.

"All that for a laptop?"

"It's what's inside that counts."

"According to you and Big Bird."

I rolled my eyes. Yep. Definitely going to be a constant thing with her. "Thanks for your help—if I can call it that…"

"Raven. My name's Raven."

I hadn't been looking for her name. I'd been looking for an insult.

"And you can call it whatever you want," she said as she closed the refrigerator door. "Just be smarter next time."

She stopped and glanced around the kitchen. Going to a pad of paper, she scribbled something, then handed it to me.

I took the paper.

She hesitated, like she was going to say something else. I wondered if she felt it too, the connection. We walked to the front of the house. She took off, heading to Salter Street. I glanced at the paper she'd given me. It had her phone number. She did feel the connection. I stuck the paper in my pocket.

Reaching into my bag, I shut off the laptop. I didn't know what kind of security Meena had on the computer, but I wasn't going to let myself get tracked. I headed for the SkyTrain and to find a quiet, dark corner where I could pry open the laptop and finally get the evidence I needed to put Meena away.

# SEVEN

Half a block from the train station, away from any CCTV cameras, I dumped the boy outfit Eagle Man had seen me in. I put on the chick outfit, made a stop at the pawnshop, then dumped the girl gear for the second boy disguise. It was complicated and annoying, but I was on my own. If Meena was looking for me, let her think I had a team on my side. I spent the night on the bench at Memorial South Park. Nothing was great about the park—at least, not from a homeless-person-needing-shelter point of view. But it sat by Mountain View Cemetery, and that was as close as I could get to the graves of my family.

At first I'd stayed away from them because of the news coverage. The last thing I needed was to show up on some six o'clock sound bite. Later, it was integrity that stopped me. Okay, maybe it was guilt. And shame. I refused to visit, to touch their graves, until I'd brought Meena down. Hunkered in a clump of bushes that helped break the chill of the wind, I pulled myself into a ball, found a sort-of-comfortable spot on the ground and let the memories of my family keep me warm.

\* \* \*

My rumbling stomach woke me early. I lay still. Light traffic, no doors opening or closing, no sound of children. The neighborhood was quiet. I stood and brushed the dirt from my jeans. My hands grazed a bump in one pocket. The money from the guy at the store. My stomach grumbled; the acid bubbled. A breakfast sandwich would be great. Coffee, freshly made. My cold fingers twitched at the thought of something hot to hold; my mouth watered at the idea of food free of mold.

Despite what anyone thought, I did have money. I kept small pockets of cash hidden in different parts of the city. But it was for an emergency. There would be no life of comfort for me, not until Meena paid for her crimes. Today, though, called for a special treat. I was close—so close— to bringing Meena down. That deserved a hot meal.

After hopping a series of buses, taking a quick withdrawal from the Bank of Jo and getting some freshly made food, I ended up on Robson Street scouting for parkades. Specifically, one with underground parking and lots of cement to block any signals from the laptop. It took a few minutes but when I saw the one I wanted, I ducked my head, pulled the baseball cap low and went for it. I took my time, headed to the lowest parking level and kept my head turned from the cameras. A sign on the wall said security patrolled the area every half hour. Nothing like a ticking clock to make it interesting.

I found a corner and booted up the laptop. The sign-in screen beamed at me, and I went for the obvious password. Her daughter's birthday. I knew it because that was the kind of employee my mom was. She knew everyone's birthdays and anniversaries, and I knew them because I used to help her shop for small gifts. I typed in the date and waited for the welcome screen.

Instead, I got a flash of red and the message *Incorrect password. One attempt remains.*

I hadn't thought she'd limit the tries to two. Visions of the computer exploding a la 007 Bond villain filling my head, I shut down the laptop and considered my options.

I only had one.

# EIGHT

My option wouldn't be around until late afternoon, so I headed to the community kitchen to see if I could pack groceries in return for lunch. Clem was there, head down, reading the clipboard. Not looking up, he asked, "Just how much trouble are you in, boy?"

"What?"

"The getup." He paused. "The hair. Who's after you?"

"How can you even see my hair and clothes?"

"Your hair's neon blond. The bigger question is, how can I not see the hair and clothes?"

I slipped my bag behind the counter. "I was looking for a change."

"And if they find you, will that change include bars?" This time he lifted his head and met my gaze.

"It's not what you think," I said. "I didn't do anything wrong."

"You can keep the wig or the clothes but not both," he said. He set down the clipboard. "Lose the wig or the clothes—" He sighed. "If it's dangerous enough, then keep the wig and the clothes, but lose us." Clem interlaced his fingers. "How big is this?"

"Been nice knowing you."

He cursed. "You can't go to the cops?" He took in my expression and cursed again. "What are you going to do?"

"I have one option."

"Only one."

"If it works, it's all I need."

"And if it doesn't?"

I didn't say anything.

He heaved a sigh. "Does this have anything to do with Amanda?"

I jerked back. "You saw her?"

Clem shook his head. "No, but after you asked, I got to thinking. A week ago, I saw her with a woman."

I waited.

"I was worried at first." He shrugged. "You know Amanda and—"

"How she made her money. Yeah, I know."

"But it was okay." Clem straightened. "At least, I thought it was okay. But if you're running from cops..."

"She was talking to one?" I asked.

"Yeah, a detective."

The room spun around me, and the world blurred, bled and tilted. I gripped the edge of the counter and held on. "You sure it was a cop?"

"She gave me her card." He reached into his back pocket and pulled out the white rectangle.

I took it, already knowing whose name I'd see, and wondering how She—Meena Sharma—was connected to the disappearance of my friend.

# NINE

Clem wouldn't let me leave until I took the hundred dollars he offered, along with his business card. "You all go missing," he said. "Keep this card in your pocket. When they find your body, I want to know."

It was the closest we'd ever get to a declaration of our friendship. "Thanks."

He handed me a Wagon Wheel. "I'd say *stay safe*, but…"

*   *   *

A couple of hours later, after a quick detour back to Vincent's, I waited outside Tron's grocery store for my option to come out. Around four o'clock, he did. The prep-school kid, blue blazer, gray pants, black shoes. He squinted at the sun and turned toward Victoria Drive. I watched him for a few seconds. The way he moved, his posture…it wasn't my place to wonder why or feel sympathy, so I shoved aside my feelings. I followed him, my mouth moving in silent practice of the speech I was going to give.

I stayed back, giving the kid space. Then I realized he never looked around, never acknowledged the world. Earbuds in, head down, he seemed to move through the streets on autopilot. Instinct had him veering left or right, avoiding the people on the sidewalk, but he never saw them. Not really. And I wasn't sure if that was good or bad, if his lack of interest would work in my favor or not.

I followed him, my brain chewing and spitting words of explanation, pleas for help. He hopped the fence and crossed the train tracks to get to the water's edge.

I did the same and waited for the moment he'd look up or stop or do something that would give me a chance to break his silent wall. But this guy wasn't in a world of his own. He existed in a solar system of one. No perfect moment. No opportunity except the one I'd create.

"Hey, buddy."

He didn't turn around.

I jogged closer. The laptop slapped my back. I stopped just short of stepping on his heels and gave him a quick tap on the shoulder.

He jerked like I'd tased him, which said a couple of things about how many friends he had and how many of them were girls. But I wasn't going to let mercy or sympathy affect me.

He kept walking.

I got in his way.

He sidestepped me.

I did it again, then matched his attempt to move around me. "I'm not going anywhere."

He stopped. Head down. Wind ruffling his brown hair.

"I need a favor—I need your type of talent, and I'll pay for it."

Nothing.

"A hundred dollars. I want you to crack the password on a laptop."

Still nothing.

"Two hundred."

Not even a flicker.

Okay, money didn't move him... so why had he been stealing it from the ATM? Of course. The challenge. "The laptop. There's only one more try left, and then it burns the files."

His gaze snapped up. Way up. I had a huge height advantage on him.

Whoa. I backpedaled. Judging from his eyes, this guy wasn't disconnected from reality or living in some la-la land. If anything, this guy was too connected, too aware. It was like he kept his gaze down and the music on so he wasn't overwhelmed by the world around him.

I moved to him. "One chance. Think you could do it?"

His focus went over my shoulder, and he moved past me. His arm brushed mine, and just like the last time we'd touched, he jerked away.

I turned my head and followed his path as he shuffled by me, and I saw the object of his attention.

Another prep-school dude. His profile was to me, but I didn't need the details to get a sense of him. Built with a boxer's frame, he was bigger, wider... deadlier than his counterpart. He stood, weight on his heels, shoulders back, hands loose, but the relaxed pose was a lie. Contained power, restrained rage. He was a coiled viper.

Too bad for both of us, I needed in his nest.

I watched him for a second, registering how he held his body, how he shifted his weight. The thing about being an artist is knowing anatomy, movement.

And everything I knew said this guy spent a lot of time in a boxing ring.

ATM Guy came to a stop beside him. The viper bent his head, leaned in close, and my impression of him shifted.

Not a snake this time. Guardian. Whatever their relationship—friends, brothers—he watched over ATM Guy with the same fierceness that I watched over Amanda. A gust of wind brought the faint trace of his scent to me: cedar and spice.

Boxer Boy pivoted with smooth precision, turned and faced me. Our gazes locked. A sharp pain hit my chest, and it took me a second to realize what it was.

My heartbeat. He made my heart beat.

Boxer Boy stepped close to the ATM kid. It was a protective gesture. And a warning.

In the back of my mind, the danger signal *binged*. But I was locked by emotions I hadn't felt in forever, chained because he made me aware of every breath I took. Just like Raven, this guy made me feel as though I was seeing my reflection.

Rule number one to surviving the streets: trust no one.

But I couldn't break eye contact with him, couldn't stamp down the feelings. We were the same, Boxer Boy and I, watchers over the defenseless. And maybe…maybe he could be the exception to the rules. Maybe…he could be more.

ATM Guy shook his head at something asked. Boxer Boy twisted his gaze from me, then put his hand on his friend's shoulder and steered him away from me.

ATM Guy ducked his head and followed in the shadow of the bigger guy.

Round one went to Boxer Boy, but I wasn't done.

My life, Amanda's life and the murders of my family rested on ATM Guy. No way was he getting away from me. Ignoring my nervousness, I hiked the bag on my shoulder and went after them.

The chain-link fence rattled as I dropped over the side and stuck my landing. Boxer Boy climbed into the driver's seat of a Lamborghini, and ATM Guy climbed in the passenger side. Thanks to Danny's love of everything auto, I knew it was an Aventador Roadster. These guys weren't just rich. They were disgustingly loaded, which meant if ATM Guy wanted to hide, I'd be screwed trying to find him. Boxer Boy put the car in gear. The tires spit dust and gravel as the vehicle took off.

Today was Friday. I had three days to come up with another plan, but I hoped ATM Guy was a routine dude, hoped Monday afternoon I'd find him at Tron's, hoped he'd help.

Too bad for me, I should have remembered rule number three: *hope* is just another way to spell *dead*.

# TEN

Saturday afternoon, I sat under the shade of the tree, far enough away from the other park goers to be left alone but close enough to feel the warmth of their lives. Pulling my knees to my chest, I took a sip of my drink and took out the fries. These were for lunch. Half the burger for dinner. The other half for breakfast.

I tried to take my time, but French fries didn't make for slow eating. They got cold too quickly. I stuffed them into my mouth as fast as I could. My intention was to come up with an alternate plan to enlisting ATM Guy. I wanted to concentrate on the problem, but something distracted me.

A dog.

No, not a dog.

A puppy.

Bulldog face, basset-hound body. She—it was a she; I knew it from the pink collar—shouldn't be that cute. It was too weird a breed mix. But the gray spots on her white body were a masterpiece to me. She was all paws and ears, running with the awkward grace of a newborn.

I was so intent on her, I didn't see the danger until it was too late. Didn't sense the predator until I had no other role to play but prey.

But he was suddenly there, silver tips on his black cowboy boots. And then he was crouching in front of me, my image reflected in his mirrored shades.

"I've seen you around," he said, his voice rough from nicotine, his nose raw from cocaine.

My survival instincts kicked in, told me to stay quiet.

"You alone?" he asked.

I didn't answer.

He smiled. "You're shy. I like that." He settled on his butt.

The fries in my stomach heaved. I'd lived through a lot on the streets—getting caught in the crossfire of gang fights, hiding in garbage cans to avoid cops. Through it all, I'd managed to stay away from guys like him. And now, because of a puppy and the yearning for a life lost—I was the fly in his web. If I wasn't careful, this guy would drain me of more than my blood.

"I'm shy too."

Not with his fists, he wasn't.

Or his belt.

Or his boots.

Or the rat.

"You look like you're all alone." He shivered as though a cold wind had touched him.

It hadn't. That's because it was howling through me.

"I can help," he said. "I've got a place." He shifted closer.

I couldn't let him touch me, and I couldn't believe I was so stupid I'd missed his presence in the park.

All because I couldn't let go of my memories, of the time when I'd been a normal kid.

"You'd have a roof—"

And walls, where no one could hear me scream.

"—and a bed—"

To turn tricks.

"—and clothes."

Stained with men's sweat and need and hatred.

"A guy like you. We could run this town."

I kept staring at my fries, smart enough to keep my gaze down so he couldn't see the relief: he didn't know I was a girl.

Relief turned to horror: he didn't know I was a *girl*.

Now more than ever I couldn't let him touch me.

A cigarette came into my view.

"Take it."

I remained immobile. It was the best weapon in my arsenal. Pimps were always sweet during the courtship. It was the "marriage" that could kill me.

He chuckled. "Real shy."

Yeah. I could see him tallying my worth. The shy boy. Worth an extra fifty bucks an hour.

"It's going to get colder," he said. "You'll want somewhere warm to stay."

It would have to be colder for me to take him up on his offer—like, hell-freezing-over cold.

"Hey, buddy."

A new voice. Deep. Confident. I kept my gaze on the fries but let my peripheral vision take over. Expensive jeans, judging by the stitching. Sneakers. Just as expensive.

"Is that your Caddy by the curb?" he asked.

"Yeah." The pimp was partly suspicious, partly irritated. "So?" The challenge rose in the question.

I felt rather than saw the second guy shrug. The wind shifted, set the leaves rustling and brought his smell to me.

Cedar.

Spice.

Boxer Boy.

Why was he here? And why was he talking to the pimp?

Oh, man. He was either going to help or make it worse.

Wait.

What if he was getting rid of the pimp not to help me, but to get me alone— alone in a bad way?

My life hovered on a sharp edge. The next thing this guy said could leave me a broken soul in the emergency room or a dead body in the gutter, and the possibilities pounded with every beat of my terrified heart.

# ELEVEN

"Think the cops are towing it."

The pimp's focus was on Boxer Boy, so I risked looking up. His gaze flicked my way. The unspoken conversation like electricity between us. I took a shallow breath as the knife's edge sharpened.

"Cops?"

The pimp twisted his head and craned his neck to squint past the trees and to his car.

Boxer Boy shrugged. "Plainclothes, I think."

Irritation squished the pimp's face. "They wouldn't tow my car."

"Oh." Another casual shrug. "Then it must be someone breaking in. Hope you don't have your wallet in it." A not-so-casual pause. "Or anything else of value in there."

On cue, the shrill beep of a car alarm pierced the afternoon.

My gaze flicked past the two guys. I could see ATM Guy on a park bench, hunched over a computer. Two guesses who had hacked the pimp's car system and set off his alarm. The pimp took off running.

Boxer Boy crouched by me, helped himself to my fries. "He's a moron." His dark eyes sparked as they flashed my way. "I'm not. First rule to pretending to be a guy—"

My mouth went dry.

"—learn how to look."

"What?" I croaked the question.

"Guys don't look at dogs like that." He nodded at the puppy. "They may want to, but they won't."

"I have sunglasses on. You don't know how I watched the dog."

"Nice try." He stood. "You're a girl. I know it. You know it." Turning on his heel, he twisted to move away.

"Wait."

He stopped, looked over his shoulder at me.

"I need your help." I rose to my feet. "Actually"—I nodded at ATM Guy—"I need his help."

"He helps me. No one else."

I ignored the hard edge in his voice, the warning in his tone. "Listen, Boxer Boy—"

His mouth quirked. "Boxer Boy?"

"You're a boxer. I know it. You know it."

"Jace," he said. "Call me Jace."

"I wouldn't ask for his help if it wasn't important."

"Yeah right. It's always important, isn't it?" There it was again—the edge, the warning. "Find someone else. He's not for rent or for sale." He turned to stalk away.

"I have an ATM kid."

"What?"

"I have someone I watch over, someone who needs protection."

Jace stared at me, then stared at ATM Guy. "You have someone you're looking after. Someone you guard. And you can't do it unless he helps you?"

"Yeah." I breathed a sigh, relieved he understood.

Jace stepped to me, crashing through my personal space until we were chest to chest. He pulled off my sunglasses and stared me down. Which was saying a lot. I'm tall for a girl. That he made me feel small underscored the difference in our sizes. Contempt scarred his face. "Then you should've done a better job." He stepped back. "Protectors don't need anybody."

He left me watching the back of him as he walked away.

# TWELVE

Raven gave me five minutes' worth of sarcasm in one glance.

"Shut up," I said.

"Did I say anything?"

Now it was my turn to lift an eyebrow.

She sighed. "For a girl who has spent two years on the streets, you're such a newb."

I scowled. "For a girl who lives on a boat, you're all wet."

She laughed, and I was surprised to find I liked the sound.

"You want revenge, don't you? Bring down Meena?"

I nodded. Today was Sunday. The night before, I'd pulled out the paper with

Raven's number, called her and rolled the dice on trusting the climber. I still wasn't sure if it was a good idea, but I needed a partner. By the time we'd finished trading secrets and stories, I knew two things. She could be trusted, and she could be a pain in the butt.

Just like me, she was carrying the need to avenge murder. In her case, it was the death of her apprentice, a kid named Supersize. It was a long story involving her drug-addicted parents and Raven seeking solace in a gang of car thieves. The main point was that she'd wanted out, and the leader, Diesel, had promised her freedom in exchange for training Supersize in the art of using urban climbing to get into the higher-end lots to steal cars. Except Diesel had set up Supersize to die in a fall. Then he'd blamed Raven.

And that had been his fatal error.

Raven was going to bring him down, and I was going to help. So was Jace, though he didn't know it yet.

"Then we get that kid to help."

Raven's voice brought me back to the present.

"And getting him means keeping Jace on side."

The mention of his name made me think of him on the park bench, the sun kissing his hair and turning the dark strands to copper and bronze. Great. Too much time on the streets, surrounded by drug addicts and pimps, had made me weak. One stupid guy with a nice smile and awesome eyes turned me into a moron. I dragged my mind from the memory of his face, the sound of his voice, and considered my plan of action.

Not plan of action.

Plan of attack.

Jace wasn't stupid.

And that was going to be a problem.

A major problem.

Unless…

\* \* \*

"You okay?"

We stood on the grass, the ocean and downtown at our backs, clouds dirty with rain scudding the skies above, and the intimidating stone edifice of Bishops Prep standing before us.

"Yeah," I said, irritated at my inability to cover my nervousness. "I'm fine." What a lie. But if I was right about Jace and his trust-fund ways, he was all about status and appearances. Going to him for help and asking privately hadn't worked. Maybe some peer pressure would help. I figured if we went at him in public, he couldn't turn us down. Not with everyone watching. He'd have to come on board. After all, what kind of guy would refuse to help a couple of girls?

"Yeah right."

I caught her smirk and scowled. Raven was strong, and I didn't like that she'd seen the weak side of me. "We gonna do this?"

Another smirk.

I ignored her.

She glanced at her phone. "Let's go. Security patrols the halls every fifteen minutes."

"That's what the student IDs are for."

Her mouth pulled to the side.

"I know what I'm doing. The IDs will pass inspection."

As usual, she ignored both me and my skills. "They catch us and these uniforms won't help."

I didn't know who the uniforms did help. Maybe the gray skirt, white shirt and red tie helped Raven blend into the school population, but I was sure I stuck out at Bishops Prep. Mostly because Raven's inside connection hadn't quite gotten my size right. The skirt was too short, the shirt too tight. I looked like some twelve-year-old boy's favorite midnight dream, and I wasn't impressed.

Two years of wearing men's clothing, of hiding my shape so I didn't attract the wrong kind of attention, and I felt every rub of the cotton fabric against my skin, every puff of air against my legs. "Wish I could wear my regular clothes."

"We have to blend in or security will kick us out for sure."

I pulled at the hem of my skirt. Raven brought her elbow to my ribs.

"Stop it. You're going to get us caught."

She didn't get it, and I wasn't going to explain.

Raven watched me for a second, then turned away. "You clean up nice." Her voice was soft.

Okay, maybe she did get it. I stopped adjusting the skirt.

Raven put her hand to the small of my back and shoved me forward. "Go."

Go. I repeated the command. Go for Emily. Go for Mom. Go for Danny. Go for Amanda. Oh man. Why were there so many names? How had my life become this...thing? I shoved the questions into the cold-storage compartment that was once my heart and stepped to the doors.

Then I took a breath, gripped the metal handles and stepped through.

The smell hit me. Or maybe the lack of it. Bishops Prep was a place for prime ministers in waiting, a place where Nobel Peace Prize winners had first grappled with quantum physics and future Fortune 500 CEOs had practiced the art of hostile takeovers. For these princesses and princes, no regular air-filtration system would do.

No. These precious ones demanded the highest air quality money could buy, and judging from the heady effects of the cool, clean air I inhaled, Mommy and Daddy were paying to have the atmosphere pumped full of oxygen, with a nitrogen boost for blood circulation.

I inhaled, then inhaled again, waiting for the other scent to hit. The one I'd come to know too well—the smell of the streets. No matter how much I scrubbed

down at the Y or how much detergent I
put in the washing machine, the scent
lingered. Despair and grime, mildew
and hopelessness—it clung to me
with the resistance and corruption of
black mold.

Raven watched me take another
breath.

All I smelled was the mandarin, cash-
mere wood and ginger of the body soap
she'd lent me.

"You going to stand there or work?"

Her words were harsh, and I wondered
if the sympathy I heard was real or
imagined. "Let's go."

She checked her phone. "He should
be in a part of the cafeteria called
Lounge A. Down the hall, to the left."

She turned in a smooth motion and
strode down the hall.

I followed her, walking slightly
behind so I could watch and mimic
her confident stride. Life on the streets
meant being an interloper in society.

I'd learned to keep my head down and my gaze averted, and I was grateful—not that I'd tell her—for Raven's company.

By the time we reached the entrance to the lounge, the small tear that had ripped my heart when I'd stepped inside the school had become a full-on gash. On the edges of my awareness, memories tingled, reminding me of a time when I was a cheerleader and an A student, when the monsters were under my bed and not in the cardboard box next to me, and security was a word I looked up in the dictionary.

"You need a minute?"

"No," I gasped. I gathered the embers of my lost life, pushed the dying coals into the dark place inside me. The task at hand needed doing, and mourning a lost life wasn't going to do anything but break me down.

I was broken enough.

Pushing back my shoulders, I said, "Let's go." I stepped through the doorway, scanning the pockets of seating areas for the guy who could help me and who I feared could end my search for justice. "See him?"

Raven frowned and peered at the mob of kids clustered in the center. "Go right. I'll go left. He's got to be here."

I did as instructed, walking the rectangular space and eyeing every kid who sat in a leather chair or lounged by the wall. A collective gasp caught my attention. I turned, curious to see what held their focus, and moved toward them.

The crowd rippled and parted, creating a space. A girl with porcelain skin and delicate features moved from the center of the circle to its exit. Taking advantage of the gap, I deked past her into the embrace of the crowd and searched to see what had everyone's interest.

I didn't have to look long.

Jace.

He sat at a table. The flat light streaming from the windows shouldn't have had the strength to reach his form, let alone edge his frame. Yet there he sat, a dark god framed in silver, his gaze focused on an ornate chessboard.

From the tight posture of his opponent, the hunch of his shoulders, I guessed Jace was winning the game.

Figured.

Slowly Jace lifted his gaze. Dark eyes the color of wild mustangs, framed by long, thick black lashes. For a long—too-long—moment we stared at each other.

Jace, looking at me.

Into me.

Through me.

Just as slowly, he turned his focus back to the chessboard, effectively dismissing me in the deliberate movement.

Jerk.

"How do you want to play this?" I asked Raven as she came up beside me.

She grinned. "Bond him."

I was hoping for something more Ravenish—like smashing his head against the table or hanging him from a tall building by his toes. Blinking, I said, "Bond?"

"James Bond." She lifted her shoulder. "Bond-girl him."

"You think that'll work?"

"He's a guy, isn't he?"

Too much of one for my taste. "Yeah, I guess." I tried to keep my voice neutral.

"You go left, I'll go right. Angel and devil. Got it?"

I frowned. "Like good girl, bad girl?"

She gave a sultry laugh. "More like bad Bond girl"—she jabbed her thumb in my direction—"and badder Bond girl." She jerked both thumbs at herself.

I'd never been bad in my life.

Raven turned and moved through the crowd, flashing a smile at random guys, then grinning with satisfaction as they gaped at her.

I pivoted on my heel and hoped I could pull off bad—or at least do a satisfactory

job of "naughty." C'mon, I told myself.
I used to date, to flirt. There was a time I'd
worn tight jeans and heels.

For Amanda and my family, I'd
channel that girl, do what I needed, take
the heat of Jace and suffer the burns sure
to come.

I got to him at the same time as Raven.

She put her hand on his right shoulder.

I followed her lead and put mine
on his left. The feel of him beneath my
fingers zapped me with awareness, and
the warmth of him made my body temper-
ature rise.

If he cared, if he noticed, he didn't
show it. No happiness. No contempt. His
indifference was as hard as the muscles
under my hand.

Raven bent close to his ear.

Oh man.

The wood and spice of his cologne was
already unhinging me. Now she wanted
me to get closer?

I was going to lose my mind. Not enough to forget about justice for my family or Amanda, but enough for me to go from Bond girl smart to Valley girl stupid. He wasn't a guy who'd respond to my flipping my hair and giggling.

Too bad.

That I remembered how to do.

Raven kept whispering in his ear, and my brain spun as it tried to come up with a plan.

Deciding to use the too-tight clothes to my advantage, I twisted to the side, popped a button, then faced forward and gave his opponent the brightest smile I could manage.

The kid stared, jerked back and blinked. Then he looked over his shoulder—probably checking to see it was really him I was aiming my pearly whites at.

I flipped my hair.

His eyes widened.

Under my hand, Jace remained motionless.

I leaned forward as though inspecting the board.

Every vertebra in the kid's neck popped as he strained to see down my shirt.

He couldn't, of course, but it was the idea that had him fixated.

Jace didn't turn his head, didn't move his gaze from the chess pieces.

I bent forward.

The kid's face went slack, and he took his hand off the chess piece he was holding.

Judging from the crowd's gasp, he'd just done something super stupid.

I pushed my mouth close to Jace. Still focused on the kid, I misjudged where Jace began and I ended. My mouth brushed the cartilage of his ear.

The kid gave a small groan.

I stifled mine and ignored the tremor of excitement that thrummed through me at my accidental kiss. "See?" I whispered to Jace. "I can help you if you help me."

That got a response.

His irritation zapped me as hot and fast as a lightning strike.

Man, seriously? Great. Between him, ATM Guy and Raven, I was surrounded by a bunch of lone wolves who'd rather bay at the moon than hunt together.

"Please, Jace—" I stopped, hearing the begging tone scratching at my voice box. "The one I look out for, my ATM kid— Amanda—she wouldn't just disappear."

He ignored me and pushed a piece across the board.

The crowd murmured its approval.

I thought of him at the park bench, the moment I thought we'd had, and I realized how totally stupid I'd been. Out for himself and screw the rest of us. It had never been about him helping me. It was just about him proving he could pull one over on a pimp. Anger simmered, bubbled.

What a loser I'd been.

And suddenly I was sick of playing Bond girl when my friend was missing, tired of pretending I belonged with these rich kids when my home was a box beside a garbage dump, and I was done with Jace and the effect he had on me.

I pushed my mouth close to his ear, not caring about the spark or the excited kick in my stomach. Told myself to forget about it. Feelings were nothing but chemicals anyway, and I'd spent a lifetime drug-free. I wasn't going to be addicted to this guy.

Ever.

And if I couldn't wow him, then I'd scare him. "Help me."

Nothing.

"Here's the thing. Your buddy? ATM Guy? He has a nasty habit of hacking the ATM machine at Tron's grocery store and helping himself to the cash."

Jace's muscles twitched.

Finally. I had his attention.

"I've got it on video," I said, hating myself for threatening but not caring if it meant finding Amanda. "You help me, or

I turn my video over to the cops." I paused to let my words sink in. "How long do you think your friend will last in juvie?"

Another pause.

"If my friend falls," I hissed, "she won't fall alone." I leaned closer, until I knew he could feel every move of my mouth against his skin. "Help me, or I will burn your friend."

# THIRTEEN

Jace had been furious, but he'd agreed to help and hold some stuff for me. I knew I'd pay—the look in his eyes had said as much. His retribution for my blackmail would be hard and swift. But I didn't care—couldn't care. Not with Amanda on the line and the chance to bring Meena to justice finally, finally within my grasp.

Another hour, and it would all be over.

ATM Guy's name turned out to be Bentley, and we—Jace, Bentley, Raven and I—agreed to meet at one of her favorite parkades on Robson Street. The concrete would block the signal from the laptop, and the busy nightlife of downtown would give us protection and decoys if anything went wrong. From here, Bentley would hack the laptop and upload the files to the Internet. Meena's life would be over.

That's what they thought.

I had a different plan. Just because I needed their help didn't mean I was willing to put them in danger.

On the corner of Burrard and West Georgia, I stopped and waited for the light to give me the go-ahead to cross the street. A gust of wind blew past. My skin tingled, and my sixth sense kicked into gear.

On cue, a black SUV, its metal shining under the streetlights, screeched to a stop. The back door flew open, and Eagle Man from a few nights earlier exploded from his seat. I shoved my arm into the other strap of my bag, twisted and ran. No way was I going to dash into traffic and risk damaging the computer. I pounded down the sidewalk, headed for Thurlow Street.

No point in yelling for help.

People dodged out of my way and almost broke bones as they dived out of his. I tried for a hard right on the corner, but Eagle Man had a long reach. He snatched me by the back of my neck.

"Didn't think you'd get away, did you, little man?"

He dragged me to the corner where the SUV waited. Wrenching the book bag off my back, he twisted my hands behind me and zip-tied them together. Then he shoved me inside. I edged to the door, tried to get out, but the child safety lock was on. He and his partner didn't talk to me as we drove through the streets and entered a parkade. We went down a couple of levels, and then the driver pulled to a stop next to a dark sedan.

Through the tinted windows of my prison, I saw Meena step from the car.

Eagle Man opened my door, dragged me out and handed her the laptop.

"Ditch the SUV," she said, her voice echoing through the empty lot. She shoved the bag onto the passenger seat of her car. "The owners have already reported the theft." Her gaze flicked to the vehicle. "Older model, no GPS or tracking...still, dump it."

Eagle Man nodded at his driver, who gunned the engine and disappeared up the ramp.

Meena turned my way, then dismissed me with a glance. "Get him inside," she said as she climbed into the sedan.

Eagle Man did as ordered, and I upped her evil cred. Whatever she did, she must be Big Bad if a Vëllazëri soldier took orders from her.

"You're stupid," she said as she started the engine and put the car in gear.

I shifted to the spot behind her seat. "Whaddya figure, Tiny?" I directed my comment to Eagle Man. "She talking to you or me?"

He didn't say anything.

"So, both deaf and dumb," I said.

"Don't be smart." Meena was smug. "You can't comprehend the kind of trouble you're in."

I laughed. "You don't know the kind of trouble you're in." Arrogance had made her stupid. Two years since she'd seen me. I'd lost weight, grown out my hair, but she should have been able to recognize me. She didn't, and it pissed me off. Rocking back, I set my feet on the back of her seat, pulled back and kicked. Hard.

Bad move.

The action lit the match on the dry tinder of my rage. Fury burned through me, lit me up. The scene in front of me became a red blur in my vision as I kicked and kicked, trying to push her seat through the windshield.

If she yelled, if the car stopped or sped up, I didn't know. The jolt of a Taser wrenched me back to the present. It set fire to my nerves, made my teeth vibrate and spiked pain so intense I felt it in my gums. I collapsed back, panting.

Meena was by the open door, the weapon in her hand, glaring at me.

Eagle Man remained in the front passenger seat.

"Don't mess with me, kid," she sneered. "I know everything, and you're an idiot. You never should have gone back to Vincent's apartment. Been tracking you ever since. I know everything." She bent forward and grabbed me by the hair to yank me upright.

My wig came off.

She yelped, dropped it and stared at me.

"Guess you don't know everything, do you?" I spun and rocked back, then, using my feet, drove all my weight and rage into her stomach. As she grunted in pain and fell away, I pulled my legs close and swung my bound arms under my hips and around my feet. Then I used her as a jumping board, stepped on her and took off running.

# FOURTEEN

Between the adrenaline in my system and the rage, I felt no pain. My legs weren't even rubbery. I ran for the ramp. Behind me, Meena yelled. Her words echoed off the cement.

A sharp, blinding pain hit my shoulders. The Taser. Another jolt of electricity ran through me. Something hard and heavy smashed my legs, took me off my feet. I fell, rolled, and the pulse in my back became a raging fire.

I didn't scream. Didn't cry.

Meena's steps rapped against the concrete, joined by the muted thud of her goon's. He grabbed and hauled me up, then dragged me back to the car. Meena followed and zip-tied my feet together. "I know you hurt," she said, "but don't worry. You won't be in pain for long."

Eagle Man pushed me into the backseat, rounded on Meena and slapped her. Hard.

She gasped at the sting and cried out when he hit her again.

So he wasn't working for her. She was working for him.

"Do it again," I said. "She doesn't seem like a fast learner."

Eagle Man's large hand went around my jaw and squeezed my cheeks tight. "Enjoy your joke, little girl," he said in a quiet, high voice. "You won't laugh for long." He shoved me back and turned to Meena. "Fix this. Now."

She didn't answer. She didn't need to—the terror in her face gave him all the response he wanted.

Eagle Man moved to his seat and slammed the door shut.

Meena gave me a hateful glare and rubbed her cheek.

"Don't be mad at me," I said. "Not my fault you can't do your job." I laughed, partly from the buzz of the pain, mostly because I knew that no matter what happened to me, my family was about to get justice.

She threw herself into the driver's seat and pulled out of the lot. "You've been a real pain. Two years of searching for you." She shifted. "Thought I was dead when I saw that video of the house fire go live. Wondered who had posted it. But when you didn't come forward"—Meena twisted around to look at me—"I figured you had your reasons for staying quiet." She gave me a triumphant smile. "Figured it was a matter of getting to you before anyone else did. And now I've got you."

I bared my teeth. "It's nice to be wanted."

"Some punk kid. This a gang thing? You trying to get in with one of the

Vëllazëri rival gangs?" She stopped at the exit of the parkade, checked for cars, then took off. "Who's initiating you?"

I looked out the window, orienting myself to where we were going. Clear night, with the car heading down Howe Street, toward the water. "You."

In the rearview mirror, her gaze flicked my way, then went back to the road. "What?"

"You initiated me, Meena."

At my using her name, she jerked the steering wheel. Her panicked gaze met Eagle Man's deadly stare.

I leaned forward and whispered in her ear: "One way or another, you're going down. Courtesy of Danny, Emily and Emma."

Her jaw went iron hard. "Nice try. But you got the name wrong."

"No, I didn't. You got it wrong." I glanced over at Eagle Man. "You screwed up hiring her."

"I'm getting that."

"You mistook Emily for me," I said. "She was a friend. I was out that night doing a junk-food run when you came into the house and murdered my family. I saw everything, Meena. Saw you go into the house. Heard the shots. Watched you run out as the flames burned. I'm a witness. What happened when the shooting started? Did you just see Emily's dark hair and assume it was me? Just decided to shoot everything that moved and hoped you got us all?"

"Josie?" Her head twisted my way. Disbelief gave way to recognition. "Why didn't you go to the cops?"

"Right. Some distraught teen's word against the word of a decorated cop. No one would have taken me seriously. You'd burned down the house—probably used a stolen gun. How was I going to prove anything? And I didn't know who else was in on whatever you were doing. What if you had partners on the force? That would've been hilarious, wouldn't it?

I go blabbing about what I saw to some officer or detective who turns out to be working with you. I'm sure they'd have been all too happy to arrange for me to have an accident while in protective custody. No. No way. I couldn't trust anyone in blue."

She stared. Processing. "But the girl—"

"Homeless kid. Off the radar. When she died, there was only me to remember her, to mourn her loss. No one else knew. No one else cared."

"Two years on the streets? You should be dead."

"So should you." I leaned back and settled in. "The night's still young." I looked over at Eagle Man, took in the anger that made his body hum. "And looks like it'll be a fifty-fifty roll which of us will die."

# FIFTEEN

In 2007, severed feet began washing up on the beaches near Vancouver, along the Strait of Georgia. No bodies, just feet. As Meena hit the brakes and we came to a stop by a deserted house that stood by the water, I wondered if my feet would become part of that mystery.

"Get her out." Eagle Man sounded disgusted. He stepped out of the sedan and took the laptop. "Find out who else she told about the files."

Three people, and they were safe in a parkade far from here.

Meena opened the car door, pulled me out, cut the ties that bound my feet and pushed me toward the broken front doors of the house. "You may as well tell me."

"Yeah, I'm all about doing your job for you."

She cuffed me on the back of my head. "Who else knows?"

I twisted, looked at her over my shoulder. "In five minutes, the whole world."

Eagle Man looked like he was going to swallow his face. "Fix. This."

Meena shook me hard enough to loosen my teeth. "Who knows?"

"Face it. You went wrong on a bunch of levels. But your big problem this time was that you couldn't go through police channels to watch Vincent's apartment, could you? Had to do it with your gang-banger buddies, and it took time to get everyone in place."

"A couple of hours."

"More than enough time to put my plan in motion."

"And look how well it worked out for you." Amusement and victory lifted her voice. "Hogtied and—"

"Hey!" Eagle Man's roar cut her off. "What is this?" He lifted the laptop. "Where's the real computer?"

Meena turned. Stared at me.

I stared back. "Who's laughing now?"

"It's a shell," he yelled. "A case and nothing more."

I shrugged. "There's a little more in it. Like the GPS tracking device from Meena's computer."

"We were tracking the wrong laptop!" He slammed the computer against the sedan and sent the plastic pieces spinning into the air. "Where's the real one?"

I shrugged. The night I'd stolen her laptop, I'd bought an identical copy at the pawnshop. Dressed as a girl, I knew she wouldn't look, wouldn't make the connection.

Meena grabbed me by the throat. "Tell him."

"No."

"He'll kill you."

"I'm already dead." I wrenched free. "I died the night you murdered my family."

Eagle Man was coming at me, and coming hard.

"Why, Meena? My mother loved you. How could you—" My voice broke. "How could you shoot her? Shoot Danny? He was just a little boy. You took everything from them. From us. And Emily? She was harmless—all she ever wanted was a home."

"I didn't have a choice."

"You set them on fire!"

"I would burn the world for my daughter!" She grabbed me, shoved me against the porch steps. "Your mom would have told you how sick Dollie is, the medications she needs. It's experimental—none of it is covered! You think I can afford two hundred dollars a pill on a cop's salary?" Her hand went around my neck and squeezed. "Where's the laptop? Tell me or they'll kill her."

Pricks of light sparked in my darkening vision.

"Tell me!"

"Let her go!" Eagle Man's voice.

Meena's grip disappeared, and I fell to the ground, gasping for air.

Eagle Man yanked me upright. "The files. Where are they?"

I ignored him, talking to Meena as I struggled to my feet. "That was my mom's mistake, wasn't it? Treating you like family, feeling like you were family. What happened? Did she use your laptop? See something she shouldn't have?"

"She didn't know—I tried to tell them she was okay—" Meena glanced at Eagle Man. "It didn't matter. I had to fix it."

"It was for nothing. She never would have figured out your connection to the gang."

Eagle Man and Meena exchanged a glance that said whatever had been in those files, it could do more than prove she was a corrupt cop.

"Where's the laptop?" he asked.

"I don't know."

He took a step, lifted his hand and cracked me on the side of the face.

With my hands tied, I had no way to hold my balance or break my fall.

He kicked me in the ribs. "Where are they?"

I retched, grateful there was nothing in my stomach to puke up. "I don't know. I gave it away." That day at Bishops Prep, I'd handed it to Jace and told him to make the files public. In exchange, I'd delete the video of Bentley. I'd told him I was giving him the computer as a sign of good faith.

That had been a lie. It was my end game, my final play.

Eagle Man stared down at me. "Finish her," he said to Meena. He moved to the car. "I'll deal with you later."

"I can find the laptop." Meena's voice rose with hysteria. "I can fix this."

He turned. Gave the cop a look only she understood.

Meena sobbed as she dragged me to my feet. "Tell me where it is."

"I don't know."

"Tell me or they'll kill my daughter!"

Meena made an inhuman sound. Her fists rained on me. She screamed at me to tell her where the computer was.

I didn't say anything, and after she'd hit me enough times to turn my vision red, she stopped. Became quiet. "We're all dead. Me, you."

I didn't say anything.

"My daughter. You'd let them take my daughter."

It hadn't occurred to me that Meena was working for the gang or that they'd use her daughter as collateral, but it was too late now. I was dead. So was Meena, and there was no way to stop Eagle Man from abducting Dollie. "You took my brother. My mother. My best friend.

One for three." I was just talking, using words to cover my pain. The thought of Dollie being hurt, another innocent victim because of Meena, another fallen child because of me… It was another black mark I'd carry on my soul.

"Let's go." She pushed me into the house. Using a flashlight, she traced the architecture. When the yellow beam landed on a column, she shoved me toward it and used the zip ties to chain my hands and feet around it.

"Why don't you just shoot me?"

"Bullets can be traced."

"You think the cops finding a body tied to a column will be less suspicious?"

"The fire will take care of the zip ties."

"Another fire, huh? There's your problem. No creativity, no imagination."

"Keep whistling in the graveyard, kid. Lots of transients here. Lots of them start fires to keep warm. It's the perfect place to end you." She hesitated. "Unless you tell me where the files are."

"Because your gang buddies will let me live? Will let you or Dollie go free? Give me a break and don't be stupid. We're all dead now. Anyway, it's out of my hands. The files have already gone public." That was the deal with Jace. Release the information on the Internet, and in exchange I'd delete the evidence of Bentley's theft. If Jace didn't do what I asked, Vincent had instructions to give the video of Bentley to the cops.

"You're lying."

"Google your name."

She did. Then she smiled. "Nothing but commendations."

My heart turned to ice as she grinned at me.

"Looks like your buddies didn't come through. Looks like I still have time to save Dollie and myself."

No. It couldn't be. Then I realized that if Bentley could hack a car system, he had the skills to find my phone and delete the video. And once that was done, Jace didn't have to help me.

*Hope*. Another way to spell *dead*.

Meena dropped the lighter and set the wood on fire. "Give my regards to your family," she said and walked out the door.

# SIXTEEN

The smoke billowed; the flames rose. I'd figured Meena's end game would look like this, and I'd taken precautions. A knife in my sock and another one in the waistband of my underwear. Only I hadn't counted on how fast the fire would move. Or how much the smoke would cloud my vision. I tried to cut the ties, but my eyes stung and my lungs burned.

I heard a noise behind me. Three figures came into view. I blinked, coughed.

Raven knelt by me, cut the ties. "Newb."

Jace lifted me over his shoulder. "Idiot."

Bentley stood watching. "The world is full of infinite possibilities," he said. "You dying isn't one of them."

"Jerks." My voice was hoarse, weak. "You tracked the laptop GPS. You were supposed to put the files on the Internet."

"While they burned you?" Jace gave me a shake. "You think we'd let you go on a suicide mission?"

"You didn't know it was."

"I knew it. You knew it." His voice softened. "We're a team, whether you like it or not." He put me in the backseat of an SUV that still had the new-car smell.

"How many cars do you have?" I asked.

"Wait till you see the clubhouse," said Raven.

\*   \*   \*

I lost track of time. When the SUV came to a stop, I opened my eyes and gaped at the view. Calling these guys filthy rich

was a total understatement. We were
in a garage big enough to need a postal
code. Jace came around to the side door.
I opened my mouth to tell him I could
walk, but he put his arms around me and
pulled me close. I kept quiet and enjoyed
the ride.

He took us to a living room that I was
sure did second duty as a football field.
The place looked like it was waiting for a
photographer from a home magazine to
do a glossy spread. It was kind of creepy,
actually. Perfect. Unlived in. Unloved.

I glanced at Jace as he walked away
and tried not to think about him and love.

A couple of minutes later, he came
back. "We need to clean you up. Lie down."

I ignored the smirk on Raven's face
and the flood of warmth that heated my
skin. The first-aid kit in his hands said he
wasn't going to go all soft and romantic
on me. I lay face down on a leather sofa
while he cleaned the cuts.

I heard Raven and Bentley talking about the laptop and going through the files.

"Payments," said Raven. "Looks like she was helping the Vëllazëri deal drugs and was helping them avoid any raids."

"There's more," I said, thinking about what Eagle Man had said about Dollie. Thinking about Amanda. "It goes beyond drugs." I raised myself on my elbows. "What now? Upload the files to the news outlets? Take it to a police station and hope some cop listens?"

Jace shot me a look. "You're kidding, right?" He took the laptop. "We send it directly to the police chief."

Raven shook her head. "Figures you'd know him."

"Wait." I moved to him, leaned over his shoulder. I went into the Sent folder of Meena's mail app and copied her address.

"Seriously?"

I ignored his question and pasted

Meena's address in the Cc section. Then, in the body of the email, I wrote, "On behalf of Emily and Danny and Emma and Amanda and Josie."

Jace gently squeezed my hand. It hurt, but it was a good hurt. A second later, I heard the *whoosh* of email being sent.

"Delivered to the police chief's private email," Jace said with a sarcastic grin. "And I thought there was no benefit to being a member of one of Vancouver's most powerful families."

Stretching, Raven said, "I helped you, noob. Remember that when I come calling in the favor."

# SEVENTEEN

A week of living on Raven's boat, and I was starting to feel human again. Even living with Raven wasn't too bad. I knew her, even the parts she didn't think I did. So when she hadn't come home the previous night, I hadn't been worried. She was smart enough to take care of herself with Diesel and the theft ring. Plus, she was hot for a guy at her school, and I figured it was just a matter of time before their connection ignited.

When the cell rang, I still wasn't worried. Annoyed but not worried. Figured she needed to be picked up. "It's six in the morning," I said.

I tried to shake the sleep from my brain and caught her saying, "Did you water Charlie?"

Seriously? She was waking me up for a weed? "Yes, I watered your plant." I paused, and then, because I knew it would annoy her, I added, "Although I'm pretty sure it's just a dandelion."

"It's a begonia, and don't you dare kill it."

I grinned as I pulled myself out of bed and moved to the kitchen. I pushed aside yesterday's edition of the *Province*. Maybe I'd get the newspaper framed. Meena's takedown had made front-page news the last few days. She was now in jail, wearing orange instead of blue. The police chief had promised a full investigation, not just into her corrupt partnership with the Vëllazëri, but also into the fire that had claimed my family. My attention focused on the sentence that let me sleep last night: "*Sharma's daughter is now in the custody of her grandmother.*" Right after the team had rescued me, I'd called 9-1-1 for Dollie. Gotten her out of the house before the gang could take her.

I kept hoping the papers would mention Amanda, how she was connected to Meena and the gang. But so far I hadn't seen anything. I wasn't going to give up. Until I saw a body, I'd keep looking for Amanda.

"Noob, you still there?"

"Yeah, what do you want?"

"Look, I called to ask you…"

Her hesitation made my skin tingle.

"I need to call in that favor."

The contained fear in her voice sent shivers down my spine. "Now?"

"Well, not now, but tonight. Is that a problem?"

"No. I mean, I never thought you'd actually admit you needed—" Wow. Raven needing help. "I mean, for sure. I'm there. How can I help?"

"Diesel, my boss, put the warehouse on lockdown."

Whoa, that wasn't good. Based on what she'd shared about Diesel and Supersize, I knew he was a bad guy. But if he was holding the kids hostage, then he was about to do something stupid and dangerous. And chances were that Raven and her crew would be destroyed. I tuned in as she kept talking, explaining what had happened to set him off, what had happened to get her to revolt. Then she said, "I've gotten everyone on board. They'll do their part. I need you to go to my school, Laurier Secondary, and talk to a guy for me. I don't have his number, and this isn't something I can ask him over the phone."

"A guy." Huh. "Just a guy, or is he *your* guy?"

Her groan told me everything, but, typical Raven, she said, "He's just a guy, okay?"

Uh-huh.

"I need you to ask him if he'll do one thing for me. I need his father to be here at the warehouse tonight. At 9:00 PM sharp. Emmett—"

That must be the guy.

"—is absolutely not to come on his own. Just his father. Tell him it's about the note he gave me. It's my reply. He'll understand."

"You want his father there? Not him? I don't get it."

"His dad's a cop."

"No," I said and felt my jaw clench. "Ask Jace."

She sighed. "I'm asking Jace and Bentley for a little help in another department more worthy of their skills. Besides, I can't send Jace to ask Emmett to help me—that will just set him off."

I knew it. "Ah, you mean Jace would make him jealous. So he *is* yours."

"Jo, can you do this for me or not? I know you have issues with cops. So do I. But I had some friends look into Emmett's dad, and if I'm going to trust a uniform… he's the best bet."

I didn't like the idea of using cops, but Raven was sure this guy would be safe. In the end, I stopped arguing. Hoped that my agreement wouldn't get her killed.

# EIGHTEEN

Jace, Bentley and I sat in yet another one of Jace's cars and watched as the cops moved into position.

"Emmett's dad's a good guy," said Jace. "The cop can be trusted." He nodded at a BMW coupe sitting at the curb. "And that's waiting for her."

As Raven had asked, I'd delivered the message to Emmett. One look at him, and I'd known exactly why Raven wanted him. Talk about tall, dark and yummy. And when he'd started talking? Oh boy. It wasn't just the deep voice; it was the attitude behind it. Yep, Raven had good taste. I glanced at *my* tall, dark and yummy and sighed.

Now wasn't the time to worry about Jace. I had enough to worry about with Raven. The plan was easy enough—if it didn't get her shot. I shifted in my seat. I had to give the boys credit: they knew how to come in force. Between Bentley's appetite and Jace's soldier personality, we had enough grub for a week and enough weapons to cover every contingency.

"It's starting," said Jace, pointing at the warehouse.

We leaned forward. The tapping of Bentley's fingers on the keyboard sounded from the backseat. Emmett's dad crept through the door of the warehouse, followed by the SWAT team.

Silence.

More silence.

Shots.

Yelling.

The door exploded open, and Raven raced into the night. She made a beeline for the car Jace had left for her. So intent on her escape, she didn't notice the goon behind her. Before Jace could act, I grabbed one of the M-32 riot guns and was out the door. Using the car door as a brace, I aimed, fired, then heard another round go off to my left.

Jace, shooting at the same time as me.

The beanbags shot from their muzzles. One hit the goon in the stomach, the other in his chest. He dropped and rolled.

A cop raced through the door and tackled the goon as he tried to stand. Raven got in the car and sped off.

"Nice shooting," said Jace.

I looked over the roof at him. "You're a good teacher, I'll give you that." The hour before we'd met Raven, he'd made me practice in his backyard—though calling it a football field would have been more appropriate.

He squinted as the taillights of Raven's car grew smaller. "And we helped give her what she wanted most. Freedom."

# NINETEEN

Jace contacted us a week later. It was our turn to help him take down his bad guy, his father, a big bad doctor who may have done something illegal. I was on board. After all, he'd helped me. Besides, it turned out that Bentley wasn't just some friend of Jace's. He was his little brother. And the more time I spent with Bentley, the more I understood the abuse, neglect and contempt he'd suffered at the hands of his father. I was all for bringing down Daddy Dearest.

So when Jace said he wanted to meet at the cannon in Stanley Park, I was all for it. The area was exposed. Since Raven didn't think Jace could be trusted, she didn't like the spot. I was pretty sure he was fine, but then again, I kinda went all Valley girl when he was around. Taking some precautions seemed like a good idea.

We tailed him to a boxing gym, watching to see what he was up to or if he was meeting anyone else. He was clean. The plan was to wait for him to finish his session, then follow him to the park. I watched the gym empty and the lights go off. No sign of Jace. We decided to go in. I figured we might find him working out.

Boy, was I wrong.

The gym was quiet, dark and smelly. I was just about to tell Raven we'd missed him when I heard Jace's voice saying, "If this is one of you two freak girls—" The name-calling didn't do anything to me, but the fear and anger in his voice put me on high alert. Raven and I ran toward the sound of his voice.

NATASHA DEEN

We found him in the men's washroom, each hand duct-taped to the business end of a curling iron. Judging from the redness of his fingers and the sheen of sweat on his face, someone hadn't just taped him to the irons—they'd plugged them in too. I went with a smart-alecky "So this is what a boys' bathroom looks like. I have to say, Raven, I've always wondered" to cover the mix of anger, fear and confusion that flooded me. Raven untangled him, and I checked out the scene of what had obviously been a hostage-interrogation situation—a notepad with questions written on it said as much.

I tossed him some easy questions, like, "Who did this?" I was sure he didn't have a clue. If he did, he'd have been after the bad guy, not slopping through the aftermath of a broken water pipe in the men's room with us. But I figured the questions were a good way to gauge if he was still mentally fit. Okay—as mentally fit as Jace could ever be. Our time to ask any serious questions about how he'd ended up in this predicament was cut short by the arrival of the Canine Unit of the police.

We escaped from the gym by making it to the roof and avoiding the cop at the back door, then ran our separate ways. An hour later we met up at Denny's. The server set three salads on the table. I'd spent two years on the streets, and this is what I got for letting Raven order for me. Limp lettuce drowning in dressing.

Raven and Jace traded words about which of the three of us was trustworthy, and I swallowed some green stuff and tossed in the occasional comment to mediate between them. Okay, and maybe stoke the fires a little.

I tuned back in when I heard Raven say, "And you're usually not an idiot. Jo and I aren't worried about your owie. The condition of your hands is significant to us for a much different reason. You show us your hands, or we walk."

At that point I put down my fork. I was having a hard enough time getting the rabbit food down. Seeing Jace's melted-to-pudding hands wasn't going to help me keep it down.

He flipped his hands over, and I took in the blisters and bubbles. "Not good," I said to Raven. "Someone was serious about getting answers from him. But in his favor, the statement on the paper was that he lied. I'm willing to assume he didn't give us up. So let's give him a chance to tell us what favor he wants from us."

"Favor?" Jace's voice was pitched four-year-old-girl high. "*Favor*? Both of you owe me. I set up the meeting to collect on a debt."

He stared at me and said, "I want you to forge a painting so we can exchange it for the real thing."

To Raven: "And once we have the real thing, you need to plant it for me."

I picked up my fork again. Whatever we were about to do, I was going to need all the vitamins and minerals I could get, and that meant finishing my salad.

# TWENTY

Part one of Jace's plan was easy. I was to lift a house key from some kid so Raven could break into the house and take a painting. That was a cakewalk. I got a Bishops Prep uniform—a boy's version— then stole the key while Jace distracted the kid with a chess match.

I spent a couple of days forging the painting from photographs. And then Raven and Jace switched the paintings. When Raven got home with the painting, she was pissed. Apparently, Jace had set us up. The house she'd broken into wasn't some random kid's. It was Jace's parents' vacation home. She wanted to bail, leave him to his own devices. Not me. I didn't care if he was playing spy games with us. He'd helped me. I was going to help him. A couple of evenings after that, we went into part two of his plan: meeting at the hospital to plant the artwork in some doctor's office so Jace could blackmail the guy for information.

We got to the hospital, and I kept watch while Raven gave Jace the lowdown on what to do. They both seemed tense, and it was hard not to catch the vibe and go all monosyllabic with them. Thankfully, they started scaling the wall and I could catch some air free of their attitudes. They climbed into the window. A little while later, Jace dropped softly to the ground beside me.

"Top of the evening to you," he said.

I opted for macho over the gooey feelings inside. "Whatever."

"Look, if it's about kicking that kitten…"

"Huh?"

"Inside joke." He sighed. "Very inside. Forget I said anything." He tugged twice on the rope. "We've got ten seconds to clear. The grappling hook is coming down."

Raven dropped the equipment, and I stuffed it into my bag, then watched as Raven turned climbing into an art form.

Halfway down, she froze. She gave a warning hiss.

A security guy, and judging by how he wielded his flashlight, he was looking to flip this gig into a job as a cop.

"Jo," Jace said. "Trouble."

"We need to distract him."

"We could make out," Jace said.

"What?"

"You know. Like in movies. We could start kissing and look all passionate, like we didn't notice the guard, and then be all embarrassed about being caught, and that would distract him from Raven above us. It's a price I'm willing to pay."

"Make out," I said. "Kiss." Jace was offering to put his arms around me... and making it sound like he'd rather take a punch by the champ. I didn't know if I wanted to deck him or let my curiosity free and take him up on the offer. Maybe I could deck him, then hug him.

"It's a sacrifice I'm prepared to make for the team," he said.

"I'd hate to make you pay a price that high," I said as I wrestled my hormones into submission. "Let's try something else." I stepped back, then started screaming, "Get away from me! I don't know you!"

"What?" Jace gasped. He stepped forward and grabbed my arm.

I didn't know if he was getting into the distraction or, unsure what I was doing, trying to get me to be quiet.

Either way, he had his hand on me and I had an opportunity to make him pay for the *sacrifice for the team* comment.

I grabbed his arm, twisted it and flipped him to the ground. And tried not to giggle at the satisfying "Oomph" of air rushing from his lungs. Standing over him, I yelled, "You're disgusting! Slimeball!" Then I turned and ran, leaving him alone with the guard coming up hard on the sidewalk.

# TWENTY-ONE

Just in case Jace was messing with us, Raven and I had decided to do some investigating of our own. So while the security guard was focused on Jace and me, Raven scooted back into the doctor's office and dug up some information about Daddy Dearest. When we handed it over to Jace, he went submarine quiet for a while, and it wasn't until I was eating breakfast and reading the paper a few mornings later that I saw how he'd gotten his retribution. Judging from the news report, Jace hadn't just looked at the files but had taken them to the right authorities. Whoever had given him the

tip to look into his father had been right.
Daddy Dearest was a dirtbag of the worst
kind. The scandal was sure to be made
into a Hollywood movie. But all I cared
about was that the jerk was out of Jace
and Bentley's lives.

"Geez, newb. What do you have?
Ringworm?" Raven tossed the jab as she
came into the galley.

"It's tapeworm, genius, and I'm
hungry."

She snorted. "You're always hungry."

I tossed the paper at her. "Look at
this."

She read the article, then made serious
eye contact. "We have to find him."

\* \* \*

Finding him was easy. Jace was at the
park, playing chess. Making him talk
to us was an entirely different game.
He ignored us, gathered his pieces and
walked away. Literally. He literally took

his toys and tried to go home. Guys can be such babies.

"We'll find you again," Raven called after him. "Might as well hear us out. Remember, you owe us. And remember, we helped you because of how often you told us we owed you."

He moved to a bench, and we each took a side.

I started the conversation. "Want to tell us about your father?"

"You probably saw the headlines," he said. "He's been arrested. What more do you need?"

"You're right." I lifted my hands in surrender. "It's your business. Not ours. I'm not here for gossip anyway. Straight up?" I said. I pulled out my phone so I could get the words on the screen right. "We're here because Internet rumors have started about a team that is"—I quoted the article—"*living in the shadows, dispensing their own kind of justice.*"

"That would be us," said Raven. "Someone sent out a message on a forum. A kid who needs help against authorities when other authorities won't help."

Jace smirked. "I think both of you need to look up the definition of *team*. Unless you mean just the two of you. If so, good luck and goodbye."

"For this kid to have any chance of retribution," I said, "we need you and your brother."

"We have our own troubles," Jace said.

"One computer hack from him, one social-situation scam from you. That's all we're asking. Then we'll leave you alone."

Jace's eyes narrowed. "What's in it for you two? Why take chances for someone else? Thought you liked being invisible."

Raven went all grown-up. "Hey, we all like to pretend we're cynical. But Jo and I realized that if you can make something better, you need to try. Injustice sucks."

"Feels good to fight it," I added. "I mean, some people recycle cans and bottles to feel good about themselves. What we're doing is just on a bigger scale. As long as we stay invisible, we can take down people like your father." I paused as I called up a text message. "Bentley's in. Are you?"

I expected him to go all lone wolf and say something sarcastic and brooding, then take off. Instead, he said, "I'm in. What do you need?"

I let Raven do the talking and since they didn't need me for it, I broke from the group and headed out. It was time for me to find a tattoo parlor and start exploring my own endless possibilities.

# ACKNOWLEDGMENTS

Much thanks to Sigmund and Judith for all the fun in creating and writing this series, and mega thanks to Andrew Wooldridge and the crew at Orca for all their efforts and support on this project!

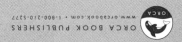

Award-winning author NATASHA
DEEN graduated from the University
of Alberta with a BA in psychology.
In addition to her work as a presenter
and workshop facilitator with schools,
she has written everything from creative
nonfiction to YA and adult fiction. She
was the inaugural Regional Writer in
Residence for the Metro Edmonton
Library Federation in 2013. Natasha
lives in Edmonton, Alberta. For more
information, visit www.natashadeen.com.